ASHWIND THE JOINING

ASHWIND THE JOINING

MELINDA CANNY

WOLF LORE PRESS

First Printing, 2025

This book is dedicated to Dr. Johnny Payne, who taught me to be a better writer and gave me the courage to put words on a page. Without Dr. Payne I wouldn't have the belief in myself to show anyone my work. Ashwind the Joining is also dedicated to my classmates Sharnell and Stacee. Without them taking the time to read my work, I wouldn't have seen the places that needed to be refined. Thank you my friends and I am happy you continue to be part of my life.

Contents

1

Chapter 1 - Secrets

Siona peeked around the alabaster pillar in the hallway just outside the library door. The ceiling was twenty feet over her head and paintings of the castle builders lined the walls.

Two ordinary students had gone in twenty minutes ago. Well, not *ordinary*, just not the *Guides*. There had to be a secret door in the library because when the Guides went in, they rarely came back out again. When the other students went in, they always came back out again.

She stood there absently wiping the same spot with her dust cloth when several students came by carrying buckets. With them was a new student, Keira, an elf girl Siona had met when she had visited the Elf Kingdom during the school break.

"Hi Keira, where does my mum have you cleaning today?"

"It's an easy one. We just have to clean the history classroom. At least it's not the stables."

Siona laughed and wrinkled her nose. Then she said, "I think she saves that for when you've been here awhile. Is everyone getting used to the idea we all have to do chores?"

Keira turned back and took a step closer to Siona. "Some people think they're too good to clean. One person told me they were going to send for their maid to do their cleaning."

A laugh exploded from Siona. "I bet if they do, the Guardian will enroll the maid in school and tell the student they have to do both of their chores."

"I better catch-up. I don't want them to think I'm trying to get out of anything." With that, Keira dashed down the hall.

Siona smiled at Keira, then her mind went back to where it had been. *I've got to find that secret door.*

Yesterday, when she had cleaned this spot, she saw three of the Guides come out of the library when they hadn't gone in. She was going to find the secret passage today.

She had been trying for days. Watching the Guides go in and out. When they saw her cleaning or hanging out nearby, they always exited the library through the door. Siona came to realize that she would have to hide in order to figure out where to find the door. She had fallen asleep yesterday waiting for the Guides to use it. That's why she had brought her dragon friend, Banprionsa, with her. If she could talk to her, she would stay awake. Besides, maybe, Banprionsa would have some ideas of where to look.

The door opened, and the students came out and ran down the hall toward the classrooms.

Siona sighed, *They're gone, so I'm going in.*

Siona, are ye sure this is a good idea? Banprionsa's words echoed in her ears. They were so shrill.

There has to be a secret door in there.

Whitfor daes it matters so much to ye?

I might find a place to hide where we can mind- talk with no one seeing me.

Siona could hear Banprionsa take a deep breath and let it out. She could almost see the steam rising. *Well, jist be careful.*

I wish you were with me.

Me too, but the village people wouldn't be too happy to hae a dragon suddenly appear.

Siona picked up her cleaning bucket and crossed over to the library door. She wished Banprionsa was by her side and not just in her mind. Aunt Erin had said they would meet soon. But that was weeks ago. She wanted to be with her dragon. Not just have these conversations in her head.

Siona, if ye describe the library, maybe Ay can help figure out where ye should look, said Banprionsa. *Wait, before ye start, eliminate all the walls that can be seen from the windows.*

Siona turned in a circle. *That leaves three places where the door could be. The space where the rolled parchments are, inside a closet, or over by the fireplace.*

Whit's in the closet?

Siona walked over to the closet and peered inside. Books stacked as high as her waist. There was no way anybody could walk through there. *Forget the closet.*

The parchments are ancient. They could crumble easily. Ay don't think the door will be near thaim, said Banprionsa. *Go closer to the fireplace and describe it to me.*

Siona walked past several floor-to-ceiling bookcases, stuffed with hardbacks. She shook her head, knowing all of them needed dusting. Then she walked by a group of small mahogany tables designed for one or two people and one giant table for group study.

Right in front of the fireplace was a sofa and her favorite overstuffed chair. She plopped down on it and tucked her feet under her. From here, she could see the entire mantle. *Wait, I hear Tristan and I think Farah's with him. I think they're just inside the door, heading toward the books. I can't see them yet.*

"What type of books are you looking for?" said Tristan.

"Something fun to read," said Farah. "Maybe a book on dragons."

Tristan turned his head and tilted his ear closer to Farah. "Dragons? Like what we saw when it banished the evil. Like the essences in our rooms?"

"Yes, and they also appear in some drawings in the cave. I just..." Farah looked down at her shoes and shrugged her shoulders.

"Let's see what we can find. Grady said he believes they lived hundreds of years ago and we know there is at least one alive now."

As Tristan went to the stacks, Siona scooted under a table and behind a pile of books so her brother wouldn't see her. *If he doesn't see me, maybe he'll use the secret door.*

Farah scanned the book titles and grabbed three. "I'll start with these. One's on dragon lore, the other is about dragons in the wars and the last is *Living With Your Dragon*." Farah grinned up at Tristan. "I would love to live with a dragon."

"If you're done, I think it's about time for everyone to meet in my room."

Tristan took the books from Farah and offered her his arm. She giggled and the two swiftly closed the distance to the fireplace. Siona moved back further, so only a hint of her face peered over the top of the books.

Farah let her arm drop away from Tristan as he limped to the left side of the mantel. He reached up between a book and the chimneypiece. Then it looked as if he tilted a small cowhide skin book and a door silently opened.

Siona clapped a hand over her mouth as she watched Tristan and Farah walk out of the library and into the secret hallway. She did a seated dance as she waited for the door to close.

Banprionsa, I saw Tristan open the door. He and Farah are going to his room to meet the rest of the Guides. I'm going to try the door now.

Siona, stop. How do ye ken none of the others won't be comin?

The rooms told me that those they picked have this stupid meeting every day. It's like they have to tell each other everything. Sometimes I hate Tristan being their leader. It's like he never has time for me anymore. But, you're right, somebody could be late and come through here as a shortcut.

He haes a big job. From whit little Ay ken, thay all do. Ay wish Ay coud meet thaim. Okay, Ay, think ye've waited long enough.

Siona walked to the fireplace. She reached for the same book she had seen Tristan move. *I'm not tall enough.*

Is thare sommit to stand on?

Siona glanced toward the tables. *I could get a chair. No, I have a better idea.*

With that, she picked up a piece of firewood and moved it to where she could stand on it. She stepped back and studied it, moved it again. *Now, if someone just glanced, it would look as if it had fallen from the pile.*

She stepped up on it and it rocked back and forth. She put her hand on the books in front of her until she was steady. Then she reached up. She was still a little short, so she moved with care on to her tiptoes.

I'm pulling on the book, but nothing happens.

Are ye sure tis the right book? Try another.

I know which book Tristan moved. You couldn't see. Wait, there's something here.

Siona moved her hand around. She could feel something protruding from the wall. *I think I found a handle. The door's opening. I'm going in.* She jumped off the log, headed into the secret passage, then pulled the door closed behind her.

2

Chapter 2– Secret Passage

Click. The door closed. Siona found herself sealed in the secret passage.

Banprionsa, there's no light.

Ga back out through the door.

Siona reached her hand out, brushing it against the jagged, dry stones. She searched for the door and then she pulled her fingers away. They had a thin layer of grit. *Nope, can't find the door. I'll keep my palm on the wall and walk forward. Maybe there will be light soon.*

Ay'm noo sure that's a great idea. Ye don't...

Her hand flat on the wall, Siona had taken her first tentative steps. *What am I supposed to do? Just sit and wait?*

As much as ye hate spiders an' mice, it might be the best idea.

Spiders aren't so bad.

Whit about mice?

Siona stopped. *You think there will be mice?*

Banprionsa's snort nearly ruptured Siona's ears. *Aye, thay'll be mice. Tis a castle that haesna been inhabited very long. And ye are in a scarcely used secret passageway.*

Okay, with a sharp exhalation of breath, Siona pulled her shoulders back. *I can do this. I won't let a little furry thing scare me.*

Are ye sure? Ay, remember that...

Stop, it was only that one time and that family of mice had tried to run up my pant leg. Oh, no.

Whit's wrong?

Emmair, I mean my mum; she made me wear a cleaning dress with boots. If the mice climb up, I won't know they're on me until they're halfway up my leg. Siona put her head in her hands and tears fell.

Siona, Siona, listen to me. Yer gaun to be all right.

Why couldn't there be lights?

Why didn't you ask? Came a gentle feminine voice from out of the walls.

What are you, like, the secret passage essence? Does everything in this castle have one?

Siona, whit are ye talking about? asked Banprionsa.

Sorry, Banprionsa, I think there's an essence talking to me. I'll let you know. But don't leave me.

Ye ken Ay willnae.

The voice came again. *Yes, I am an essence. I am Lil, from The Lion Room.*

You're the Princess, the one who went deep into the earth to save herself.

Yes, and I know, though most don't, that you had a hand in saving me. So, what is it I can do for you, little princess?

I'm not really a princess.

Did you not see the Elven King? And did he not proclaim you a human girl, a princess of the elves?

Yes, his daughter Aine, I'm not supposed to call her Princess. It's a secret. She asked him too. So, King Arlen, he made me one and even gave me a crown with real jewels. But Prince Ainmire, that's Aine's uncle, said I needed to leave it with the elves until I was older. So Aine, she made me a crown of flowers and used magic on it, so the flowers are always fresh. Laughter bubbled from Siona as she spoke into the air.

Take a breath, you talk much. Now, little Princess. Is it light that you need?

Yes, I don't want the mice to get me. With that, the torches in the hallway lit up and, though there were still shadows, Siona could now see. *Princess Lil, are you mad at me for being here?*

The sounds of laughter echoed off the walls. Siona realized it wasn't just one person's laugh, but several.

No, Princess. We were expecting you. Now I will let you search for your place. For I fear if I just show you, it won't mean as much. There was a pause and Siona was just going to speak when Lil's voice came again. *Besides, it's fun to explore.*

Siona, who wur ye talking to?

She put on the lights. I can see everything.

Okay, but who?

Princess Lil she created the Lion Room and picked Tristan to be her champion. She didn't even care that other people think he's a cripple. Well, it's not her cause she'd be really old. It's her essence.

Right. She left a piece of herself in the room when she created it. Noo jist her, but her dragon too.

We don't want to forget the dragon. I wonder if her dragon was her best friend, too. Siona knew she had said the right thing when she heard Banprionsa sigh. *Now, let's explore.*

Next time, I'm bringing a torch that I can light from the ones on the wall. That way, I can go in any direction.

Siona came to a junction. There were lights both ways. One way, she could see what looked like doors. She decided those must be to the Guides' rooms. Siona turned the other way and walked. When she was halfway down the corridor, the lights flickered and went out. Siona heard a noise of something slithering along the wall. Then she felt like she was in a shower, but instead of water, it was steam.

Banprionsa the lights went out and there is something very large coming at me.

Move as far to one side as ye can.

Which side?

Can ye tell where the thing is coming from?

It seems like it's all around.

Then jist pick a side. Sit down and make yerself as small as possible. See if the essences can help ye.

I'll try. I wish you were here.

Siona put her back to the wall and pulled her knees to her chin. She tucked her head down so only the crown was visible. She folded her arms around her knees to get them in as tight as she could. The slithering had stopped. The steam bath hadn't. Siona gulped in air, trying to keep a sob down.

Princess Lil, are you there?

The creature could smell something that it had only had whiffs of. It swung its head back and forth. He had his body armor in place. Ready to face down whatever had invaded his home. Its head met something soft and malleable, Siona's arm. The creature and Siona both let out a high pitch scream. It was unclear whose was shriller. The screams would have brought people from all over if they could have heard it. Siona felt more scales as the thing slithered by her, racing away like it was being chased by wild fire.

A chorus of laughter echoed off the walls.

After not feeling anything for a few seconds and the temperature returning to normal, the torch lights came back on. Siona still kept her head down, even after she knew there was light. She was sure the creature was just a few feet away, and she didn't want to see it. Maybe if she just sat here and not move it would really go away.

Princess Lil, are you going to tell the girl?

Alright Riley, Siona, the lights are back on.

Lil, that is not what I meant and you know it. The child is terrified.

Siona, you are a princess, and princesses don't huddle in corners. Get up and keep looking or you'll have to look again tomorrow.

Siona shuffled to her feet and started back toward where the Guides rooms were.

Little Princess, turn around and go the other way.

But Princess Lil, I don't want to run into that creature.

He's gone for now, but the two of you are going to have to learn to get along.

What is he? asked Siona.

Something else for you to figure out, young one. Just know that while you are down here, we guard you and nothing that lives in our castle will hurt you.

Siona, are ye alright? asked Banprionsa.

I guess so. Princess Lil says I have to figure out what that thing was on my own. For now, I'm going to keep looking for the room they want me to find.

Siona glanced further down the way and she thought she saw doorways. She moved toward where she thought the door was, but it wasn't there when she arrived. She looked and saw another door and moved to it. Same thing. She went to a third and again it had vanished.

Siona decided she would talk to the essences again. Hoping they would be more helpful than they were with the creature.

I know I saw doors; how come I don't see them now?

It's not your door to open. Keep walking and you will find your door, said the essence of Lil.

Siona stopped. *Did you just say my door?*

Yes, little Princess, I did. Lil said, the laughter bubbling up as she looked over at Caratenga. *We've been told you need a place to practice, so we are providing you with one.*

Practice what? said Siona, still not moving. *And who told you I needed one?*

Your dragon talk, said Lil. *Aunt Erin did before she left. But if you don't start moving, we might change our minds.*

Siona felt a wind rise, and it was as if a hand touched her back, then pushed her forward. She stumbled, and she didn't know why or how she hadn't fallen. Then she looked up. There, at the far end of the tunnel, appeared the outline of a door. Siona thought there was a dragon carved into the front panel. She ran.

When she got to the door, the dragon glowed the color of rubies. Siona reached for the handle and pushed. Nothing happened. Then she backed up and looked at it more closely. She stretched and rubbed the dragon carving like it might be a magic lamp. Again, Siona tried the door. Still nothing.

If this is my room, how come I can't get in, said Siona.

You haven't asked to enter, came the reply from a voice Siona didn't know.

If you say so. Dragon Room, may I enter? Siona said.

With that, the door opened and Siona stepped through. She found herself in what appeared to be a small room, and Siona wondered what she could do in such a small space. Then she noticed a ruby-colored light and moved toward it. It led into a larger room. She realized she had been in a closet.

Siona made a circle around the room. There was a bed, exactly like the one she had slept in the night she had stayed in Tristan's room. She saw a window with a seat built-in that overlooked Dragon Alley and the house she lived in. On one wall was a desk with a carved chair like the neck of a dragon; its eyes appeared to follow you.

Siona, you need to understand a few things. Can you sit and listen for a minute? said Lil.

Siona walked over to the window seat and sat with her legs dangling as she faced into the room. *Yes.*

First, tell nobody about this room, said Lil. *Can you do that?*

I won't tell.

Next, the only way into this room is through the entrance you just came in. If you enter the secret hallway and somebody else is there, they won't see you unless you talk to them.

I'll be invisible?

Yes. Last, you can only come here when you have finished your chores. The door will not open if you haven't done them. You also have to say these words, Labhraím le dragain.

Siona nodded and repeated the phrase to herself over and over. Then she said, *Do I get to talk to the Dragon Essences that live in the rooms?*

A chorus of *yeses* echoed through her room.

3

Chapter 3 – Siona and Banprionsa

Banprionsa stood with her friend, Tuarcleite as they watched the hatchlings cavorting on the flame-colored sand, tear through the woods like sprites, or soar over the azure seas reaching out to play tag with the frothy tips of the waves, she noticed that as they played the children watched.... waited... listened...

Ye are so much better at watching thaim than Ay am.

Tuarcleite gave Banprionsa a shove. *That's because ye want to ken whit's gaun on up thare. Ga on. Just come back and tell me whit ye find out.*

Banprionsa turned to where the adult dragons had gathered on the granite plain with its deep ruts of obsidian glass. *Thanks, normally thay'd be talking about our pranks.* As she moved closer, she turned back to her friend. *Today though, Ay thinks tis about the fact that the rooms of Ashwind Castle hae selected the Guides.*

The council had gathered in front of the mouth of the dank cave. Their argument Banprionsa knew would go on for a long time, and it would be like circling vultures over a carcass. Even from where she stood below the cliff, she could hear most of the questions they bellowed. They spoke without waiting for any answers.

Are ye sure it is the hour?

Have the Guides actually gathered?

Ay thought the leader was missing.

Sighing, Dubhbragh, the eldest of them all, extended his crimson head and roared, matching flames shooting up through his nostrils. *Silence, says Ay! Silence!*

The reverberation was so loud that the trees shuddered. The young ones froze in their play and gaped as they waited for what would happen next.

Banprionsa's talons rooted her, like the surrounding woods were rooted to the earth. The orange and black feathers on the nape of her neck stood straight up. She had never heard her adopted father sound so angry. Banprionsa knew she didn't want to miss anything being talked about. She moved silently under the rock that jutted out from where the adults were standing. As she moved forward, Siona breathed into her mind.

Banprionsa, I have something to tell you, said Siona.

Can ye wait? The elders are speaking.

No, but I'll be quick. The Guardian has asked the dragons to come. We are finally going to meet.

Ay thought that was what thay were arguing about. Ay need to get closer, so Ay can hear.

Let me listen too.

Okay. But stay quiet. Or Ay might not catch everything.

With that, Banprionsa again moved slowly to situate herself right under an overhang. She knew precisely the place to go to hear all that was being said, but she also knew the least noise would echo from this spot and she didn't want to get caught.

Banprionsa, where are ye gaun? asked Searteanga.

Jist gaun to sit for a minute.

So, ye want to hear the argument.

Banprionsa waited, holding her breath, as Searteanga moved stealthily, his pebbled pale purple breast scales barely grazing the obsidian. He crowded in next to Banprionsa, causally draping one leathery wing across her back. She tried to draw away, but there was no room. Her back feathers ruffled while her throat scales blushed an angry tangerine. He didn't care what the discussion was about, he just wanted to know what interested her. Banprionsa tried to ignore him. She turned her head away and closed her eyes.

If she wanted Siona to know at the same time as her, she had to picture the blue- eyed, blond-haired, two-footed girl. Then she had to concentrate on conducting the message as she heard it. Like keeping her eyes open when she sneezed. It wasn't easy. Normally, the two just talked between themselves, mind to mind. Her dearest wish was to get to meet Siona not only in her mind, but in the flesh. She was lucky to have found a dragon talker in the ether before they had come to this place. There they became linked and nobody could tell either of them differently.

Banprionsa knew, from what Siona had said, that Siona had learned quickly, not to mention their connection. People had looked at her strangely in Siona's old village, even before she and her two brothers had become orphans. Now that Siona was in Ashwind Village with a family that had adopted them, she didn't want them to think she was strange. That they might send her away was her deepest fear. Banprionsa knew she was careful whenever they communicated.

Ay hae listened to the Guardian. He says all the Guides hae congregated. He requested we keep the pledge we made faur back, said Dubhbragh. His regal bearing showing as he stood to his full height, his long neck uncurled as he swiveled his head to eye the elders. His scales cooling to a more temperate hue.

Fadcruba stood up and walked to the center of the outcropping, his scales the color of marigolds shone brightly in the afternoon sun. He had his leathery wings tucked neatly at his side.

Ye want hus to honor a promise made hundreds of years ago. When the others went off to find what thay needed, leaving hus here alone to guard the borders. Hae not come to visit, but the Guardian. Whitfor, should we leave our home now for elves, dwarves and humans?

Did ye hear? asked Banprionsa, *Ay declared. The Guides returned. Ay told you that Ay could speik with my rider.*

Aye. Ye hae been saying that for years! said Searteanga.

Suddenly, Siona popped back into Banprionsa's mind. She interrupted the conversation between the two dragons.

I wish I could see everything and not just hear it. Is that possible?

Ay'm going on top. Ay need to see everything to ken completely. Banprionsa communicated what she planned to do to Siona and explained she might not speak to her after they moved.

Ye know thay don't want us up there. Never hae Ay known ye to break the rules, said Searteanga.

Well, this is different. Ay will inform ye of whit Ay learns.

With a groan, Searteanga followed the smaller dragon as she scaled a nearby tree and then silently glided from treetop to treetop until she perched on a limb that overhung the entrance to the cave. She stayed concealed in the pine's crown, her sharp ears focused on the conversation below. The elders were arguing about the agreement.

Fadcruba, ye know that we agreed to stay here while they went to find the supplies needed to build a new world. Yer grandfaithers signed the agreement, and tis binding today.

Dubhbragh, only ye say tis binding. Most of hus want nothing to do with the two-footed races.

Then there was a mixture of raised voices from both sides.

Ay want to hae a rider. We hae to go.

Thay've ignored us, think we are myths. We should leave it that way.

We agreed.

No, dead ones agreed. Ay d'noo.

Yer faithers, fatihers agreed to this covenant, and now ye want to discard it like pieces of auld meat. Ye dishonor yerselves and yer tribes.

Whitfor should we believe the Guardian? said Fadcruba.

He haes never lied to hus. Whitfor would he now? The dragon talkers are at the castle too, said Dubhbragh.

If dragon talkers wur thare, we would ken. Some of hus would hae made contact.

Ach, but one haes. Ask Banprionsa. We hae all heard her talk about a blonde human girl wee ane that she needs to be with. Is this not the proof ye need?

Banprionsa haes been claiming this for years, said Fadcruba as he snorted a puff of smoke. *Now ye want hus to believe she can do something that the rest of hus canna?*

Hearing this, Banprionsa went immobile. The scales of her breast glowed an angry crimson. She knew her rider was there and that the child was a dragon talker she had known since the day she and the human girl were born. They had been communing from birth, though nobody believed her... well, Dubhbragh did. The others had just made fun of her, telling her she just wanted a make-believe friend. But she knew that two others also felt the pull. They just didn't talk about it. Now they were saying they might not go. Well, she didn't care. She might be one of the youngest, but she would go even if she went alone.

Instead of fighting, let's meet back here when the sun dips behind the volcano. Bring whoever ye wish. We will look into the pool of knowledge, and ye will see what goes on at Ashwind and decide ef we should go there, said Dubhbragh.

Banprionsa, you must come. Don't let them keep us apart anymore, said Siona.

Shouldn't Ay wait until the elder's council haes finished their meeting tonight?

Don't you think it would be best to leave while they talk? That way, they will be too busy to notice that you have gone. Please, please Banprionsa.

4

Chapter 4–To Ashwind

Ay hope Ay'm doing the right thing. No, Ay ken Ay'm doing the right thing. Tis time for Siona and Ay to meet.

Banprionsa knew that there were two other dragons who talked to riders, though she realized they kept it a secret. She knew they did because over the years she had seen them in private moments. They would have the same look on their faces she had on hers when she talked with Siona. Banprionsa went to find them. She wanted them to go with her to Ashwind Castle. Banprionsa was certain that there was no way their sires would let them go. She swooped down from the hillside and gathered them. She kept the gossipy Searteanga with her, so he couldn't blab to anyone else about what was happening.

She told them what she had overheard and asked the two to join her on the trip to Ashwind. Each of the others wanted to bring one of their friends with them. So, they hurried off, searching through the caves until they assembled their companions. Everyone agreed to go, though they thought her reason was crazy. For them, it was a chance to experience a world that was forbidden. Most had no genuine belief that there was a rider waiting.

Banprionsa didn't care why they would go; she was just glad that the eight of them would head off as the sun dropped behind their volcano. The adults would be in conference then, and she knew they would argue for hours. This would give them the start they needed. She hoped they would arrive at Ashwind and not have to return.

Siona?

Yes, I can hear you.

We will be on our way shortly.

When the adults went into the cave's inner sanctum, the young ones started out. The sun, cringing in anticipation of the fireworks to come, had just cast its last glimpse over the rim of the volcano. The children took the water's edge, following the shore's outline. Some flew, others hopped, glided or burrowed underground. They kept watch to be sure they left nobody behind. Traveling in pairs, no member of the group was ever out of sight of the others. As the moon rose, the familiar landscape took on a different feel. Some dodged among the trees, while others tried to block out the light of the moon. The boys wrestled each other in midair, seeing who would fall the closest to the ground before pulling up. The girls laughed, telling them they would leave their crushed skulls exactly where they hit. They knew they had to continue traveling from dusk to dawn, to keep hidden during the daylight. That way, neither the two-footed ones nor their elders would see them.

Banprionsa contacted Siona and allowed her to see through her eyes where they were and what they were doing. When she did this, it took all her concentration, which left her with a headache. She knew she could only do this a little each day.

Wow, look at the stars, they are so bright out where you live. Are those boy dragons who are wrestling? Siona said.

Aye.

So even boy dragons aren't very smart. I have to go now. I need to get a little sleep or I won't be able to do lessons tomorrow.

Will speik again on the morrow after night falls. Ay willnae be able to show ye pictures. It will be too dark.

They traveled for hours and finally called a halt to hide during daylight. Banprionsa smiled as she looked at the assembled group. There was a member of each tribe here. *This should make the elders come.*

Banprionsa's mind rang like the time she had fallen from a pine tree and hit the eagle rock. It was Dubhbragh. *Oh, boy, he must be orange; he sounded like he was spitting fire.*

Banprionsa had learned as she grew what all her adopted fathers' colors meant: robin's egg blue - happy, gray - melancholy, red - enraged, orange - upset or annoyed. Purple, her favorite, was when he tried very hard to scold her, but was really struggling not to laugh.

Where are ye? Ay know ye aren't in camp! D'noo shut me out, ye haven't mastered that, Dubhbragh said.

Faither, Ay'm in a cave. Some of us went on a camp out. Sorry Ay d'noo tell ye.

Right, how many have gone on this 'camp out?' Could it be eight of ye?

Yes, faither! How did ye ken?

Banprionsa, ye and the others need to come home RIGHT NOW!

Hm, Ay have to go now. The others are trying to sleep, and yer shouting at me is making my brain hurt. Bye Faither! Ay will see ye soon, Banprionsa said. She closed her mind to Dubhbragh as she had practiced.

As she looked around, she saw the others staring at her. *Thay ken.*

The sky glowed a golden orange as they launched this, their last night of flight. They left the cool ocean breeze and headed inland toward the mountains. As they swooped over the ocean, they had their last glimpse of the blue florescence deep within the waves crashing against the shore.

Within their first hour of travel, they passed several villages. Each unique in their layout and color. The first had houses that circled a town court with rows of corn and wheat growing beyond the pastures. The houses glowed soothing amber. Another larger hamlet had larch lined lanes leading to a large lodge whose lustrous lamps glowed like luminous lava.

Siona, are ye thare? Banprionsa said.

I'm here.

Ye sound concerned.

The Guardian knows about us. He gave me a message for you.

He kens? How?

I think your Papa told him.

Oh, Ay'm in trouble.

I don't think so. The Guardian didn't seem very upset. Though he tried to look stern. He told me to tell you it might be best to go home.

No!

I told him that wasn't possible because we had to meet.

Ye d'noo.

He just nodded and walked away. I asked where you should land, and he said you would have to ask your father.

Ay will have to think about this. With that, Banprionsa raced to catch up with the other dragons. While Siona raced into the house for supper.

The young dragons soared above hills that over watched a valley sheathed in darkness. Pulling up into a stall, for a moment, the dragons could see the moon reflecting off the white foam of the waterfall as it plunged into the lightless depths of an unseen tarn. Banking to the right, they plummeted into the gloom of the valley below. Zooming along the river, they glimpsed Ashwind Castle with its pennants flying over the parapet lit by witch lights. The young ones drifted on the wind as they decide how best to approach the fortress.

Faither, may Ay talk to ye?

So, Banprionsa, ye want to speak with me now? Ye couldn't have talked to me before ye ran off without a thought of what might happen? Where are ye? said Dubhbragh.

Ay am almost at Ashwind. We should arrive there by first light. Um, what should we do? Would ye tell the Guardian we are comin and ask where we should land?

Hm, why don't ye wait for hus to catch up? We are only a couple of hours behind.

The others might not let us go on, and we have come too far. Please ask the Guardian for me, please, Faither. I don't want to have flown all this way and not make it. Ay need to meet Siona. We need riders. Ye know better than anyone how much we have missed because we don't have thaim. Please Faither, we will land somewhere in Ashwind, and Ay don't want to scare anyone. Ay know ye are angry, but...

Stop...

Banprionsa stalled in mid-flight; smoke flowed slowly from her nostrils. Her scales turned anxious indigo as she waited for a reply.

He says to go behind the castle where lays an open area. He will be there to greet you. G'luck wee ane, see ye soon, Banprionsa ye and the others will come before the Elders Council to answer for yer transgressions.

5

Chapter 5 –The Long Awaited Meeting

It was just before the sun woke for the day when Banprionsa and her friends arrived in Ashwind. The town still slumbered as they moved behind the castle to where, long ago, the Guardian had made dragon alley. Banprionsa knew from what Dubhbragh had told her that this was where dragons and riders could live and train. There was a wide-open space, the size of ten of the tallest pine trees laid end to end, that would allow for easy take-off and landings. Enormous pathways, through the forest that surrounded it, led into the mountain. The cave entrances were clear, and inside was a maze of tunnels that led throughout the mountain. Each had rooms that would comfortably house a dragon and a rider. The Guardian had always made sure they kept the area up, but the people did not understand why, as they only used it during the annual festival. As the dragons arrived on air and land, they saw an old man holding the hand of a singularly diminutive blond girl. The others turned to Banprionsa, most with incredulous looks on their faces. Her best friend Tuarcleite came up next to her, smiled. Then she said, *Banprionsa, this is so cool.*

The young dragons stopped several hundred feet from the Guardian and the girl, Siona. Banprionsa could see that Siona was pulling on his hand to let her go. Banprionsa was sure that Siona wanted exactly what she did: to touch the one who had shared her mind and soul since before birth. She was equally sure the Guardian was worried about not frightening the other dragons.

"Wait, child. I understand what you want. However, the proper greetings need to take place. Give us a chance. If I let go of your hand, will you stay still? If not, I will send you back to your bed, where you should still be."

Banprionsa moved forward with care. Ay *started this, and Ay am Dubhbragh's dochter. Tis up to me to greet the Guardian, the rider of my faither. Ay need to show the proper respect and ask his leave to remain in his lands.* As these thoughts went through her mind, her steps became bolder, even if her legs continued to tremble. She looked first to the Guardian and then to Siona, though she glanced back, as was proper. She looked directly into his bottomless chocolate brown eyes.

Ay stand Banprionsa, dochter of Dubhbragh. Ay ask permission from ye, the Guardian of Ashwind, to allow hus sanctuary within your lands. We come to fulfill the agreement of the covenant that was made long ago. Under this agreement, once the essences selected the new guides, the dragons would rejoin the two-footed-races. Her eyes never leaving the Guardian's face and her voice only trembling once or twice.

Welcome Banprionsa, daughter of Dubhbragh, for whom I hold great love and respect. You are welcome on this land until the elders of your race have arrived. They have informed me of your rather rash behavior. Which your parents will deal with when they reach here. Though I am happy to see you, there is still much to be decided before I can grant sanctuary. Banprionsa opened her mouth, but the Guardian held up his hand to stop her.

While we wait, you and the others are my honored guests. I ask only that you stay in Dragon Alley until I can warn the rest that you are here. For most, it will be a great shock. For others, a welcome surprise. Now I believe there is someone here that wishes to greet you. Yes, Siona, you may go now.

Siona and Banprionsa danced toward each other. Each was so happy finally to see the other in the flesh, the others watched in wonder as the two silently greeted one another. They stared in wonder when Siona touched Banprionsa and she glowed brighter than the sun. They still only communicated in their minds. Everyone so focused on those two that they did not heed the shadows or notice the ones that were hidden there.

***

The Guardian didn't realize there were any humans outside the Guides and their friends who knew that dragons existed. These others that knew were the Followers of Purity, or FOP. Two children were elite members of the group, Carin and Nessa.

Nessa stood staring at the dragons for a moment, then she turned and, eyes flashing, looked directly at her cousin, Carin. "Why did they have to show up now?"

The FOP believed only humans were good enough to bond with dragons, that the dwarves and elves needed to be kept in their places. Dwarves should stick to being miners. Elves should tend the trees and animals. They wanted both groups to have their magic stripped. They were abominations, those who had inter-bred. Vile creatures that the Gods had never intended to live. The FOP wanted them killed.

Carin and Nessa, cousins and among the youngest members of the group. The idea had been for them to be selected as guides. When that failed, they had been told to stay at the castle as students. Their job was to recruit more members for their group. Secondary to that was to report back when the dragons arrived at Ashwind Castle.

In order to recruit others, they also had to pretend to be friends with all races so they could cause trouble from the inside. Carin had recruited some of the other boys. While Nessa, always shy, had tried to be friends with the girls, but found it challenging to keep her disdain for the other races to herself.

The shadow dwellers moved swiftly away. "Nessa, you were right. She's a dragon talker," said Carin.

"Quickly, we must tell the others before they can ruin our plans."

"I'll go. You go back to the castle and make excuses for me, in case I'm not back when lessons start. Nessa, you're much better at making them believe you than I am."

***

After greeting Banprionsa, Siona reluctantly went home to wake her brothers and her new parents. The dragons were here, and she had to tell them as soon as possible. She had known for months that both Ryuu and Pogee were dragon talkers. She had seen them when they had not realized she was there. *Why did they all think they needed to keep it a secret from each other and their parents and other siblings?*

After waking the part of her family who lived in the Guardian House, Siona decided she would go tell her older brother Tristan. Tristan stayed in the castle as the essences had selected him as the leader of the Guides. She had been happy for him and had always known he was special. He loved her fiercely, he always protected her and at least pretended he believed Siona talked to a dragon. Siona knew he would be happy for her. She also knew he would tell the other guides, especially her other adopted siblings. Siona started around the corner and was so excited that she didn't see the lurking shadow. Before she even had time to holler for help, he had used a magic word that hushed her mind and mouth.

6

Chapter 6 - Taken

Banprionsa watched as two boys rounded the corner from the house she had seen Siona go into. These must be Pogee and Ryuu. She watched as they stopped in their tracks. Then she saw them turn this way and that until each found the dragon they sought.

The first to move was Pogee. She knew because Siona had told her he looked like a beanstalk. Siona had been right: he was skinny with a shock of hair the color of a carrot. Then she heard him call, "Gormcleite, is that you?"

Banprionsa watched as Gormcleite, a young female blue feathered dragon, moved toward the sound of Pogee's voice. It surprised Banprionsa that the Gormcleite was more than three times the size of Pogee. If it was anything like her experience with Siona, she knew that Gormcleite's heart was pounding so loud it drowned all other sounds.

Then she saw Glascruba, who was only a little taller than her friend, open her leathery wings as she moved toward the short stocky boy whose hair was the color of honey. Ryuu was his name, and he was Siona's biological brother. Banprionsa shot a short bit of fire into the air with happiness.

The four stood together and talked like the old friends they were. Each boy had talked to their dragon counterpart from the time they were babies. While Banprionsa kept staring at the spot where the boys had come from. Finally, after several minutes, she joined the group. *Do ye ken where Siona is?*

I bet she went to tell Tristan. She always wants to tell him everything, said Ryuu.

Hm, the dragon burbled deep in her throat. *Ay hae been calling for her, but she has not responded.* Her scales turned indigo as she looked at the boys.

Get used to it. She does that to us all the time, Pogee said. *Mum says she only hears what she wants to.*

Banprionsa rejoined the larger group, still alarmed that she couldn't reach Siona. It was like what her father had told her happened when a rider died. It was like her soul had fled the world. She felt emptied. Though she was sure Siona wasn't dead, she could still feel a small spark deep inside. She knew that something bad had happened, but none of the others seemed concerned.

"Pogee, Ryuu, what are you doing?" shrieked Emmair, their mum. "Get over here right now."

"Ah, Emmair, I see you have found our honored guests," said the Guardian.

"Guests?" Emmair threw her arms in the air, then pointed toward where the boys stood. "They're dragons, or they look similar to the fairy tale dragons from books, but lots bigger."

"Ah yes, where is Siona? I thought she would be back out here by now," The Guardian said, peering over Emmair's head.

"She probably went to tell Tristan that her imaginary friend isn't imaginary," said Ryuu.

As he shook his head, a look of concern passed over the Guardian's face. *Banprionsa, call to Siona and tell her to get back here. We have much to discuss.*

Shaking her head, as the indigo of her breast-scales drained leaving them a muddy blue fairer than the palest lupine, Banprionsa softly told the Guardian, *Ay hae been trying, but she haesna answered. It feels as if her soul is fading.*

The Guardian stood like a tall oak tree. Only his eyes darted from one corner of Dragon Alley to the castle and then over toward the caves. He was glad that their new dragon friends preoccupied the boys. Only he had tuned to Banprionsa and heard what she had said.

Just then, she saw a man walk around the corner. It must be Cadryn, Siona's adopted father. He didn't seem surprised after his first startled glance. Banprionsa thought maybe he, too, was a Dragon Talker. As he slowly sauntered toward the Guardian, his eyes never left the dragons. It looked as if he were searching for someone.

Cadryn approached the group, and Banprionsa was sure he recognized the color of her worry. She was certain of it when he spoke.

What's wrong?

Siona has gone missing. It surprised me she's not here with her dragon. Now Banprionsa says she can't reach her. The boys thought she went to see Tristan. But that doesn't explain why her dragon can't contact her, said the Guardian.

Banprionsa watched as Cadryn turned toward the boys. She could see the worry that had crossed his face. "Boys, go up to the castle and bring Siona back here. If you can't find her, bring the others back with you. I want her found."

"Papa, you know how Siona is. She goes where she wants. She'll be back when she is ready," said Ryuu.

Without moving a muscle, Cadryn projected his authority in a way that even the dragons on the other side of Dragon Alley felt the power and authority. "Boys, do as I say now! Find your sister."

Though the boys took off at a run, with Banprionsa's sharp hearing, she heard them grumbling about little sisters being a nuisance and always in the way. Then she saw Emmair running toward them. Banprionsa felt her fear running over her like water from the falls.

"Now Emmair, don't worry. We just want Siona here with us and her dragon can't seem to talk to her."

"Her dragon?"

Guardian, pray tell the mither of Siona that Ay ken she is still alive. Ay can still feel a small breath of her soul. Though something is in the way.

Cadryn jumped slightly as he realized he understood the young dragon. The meaning of the dragon's words overwhelmed his surprise. *Oh gods, this was not good.* He had learned as a boy what that meant. He knew Siona wouldn't be coming around the corner soon, if ever.

Though Banprionsa knew better, she still hoped to see Siona barreling around the corner of the gray brick wall that embraced the castle. She had paid little attention when she arrived, but now she studied it, anything to keep her mind from screaming with the silence. In each of the four corners of the castle, there stood a parapet. They were as tall as the fir trees that blanketed the mountainside. The castle was encircled with a rampart where, here and there, groups of children and young people were gathered, peering down at them. They had made the castle from blue-stones, the color of a mountain jay. The grass here was soft, unlike that which grew near the volcano, which mimicked the prickles of a porcupine.

Banprionsa heard Ryuu shouting as he careened around the corner, "Father, Siona is not there. She never saw Tristan. We brought him and the others."

Tristan limped over to where the Guardian, Cadryn and Emmair were standing. Banprionsa saw fear leaking from his eyes. She knew this was the sister who he protected. That he had watched over her and Ryuu while they lived in the village, always making sure that they had food and shelter. Though they were all adopted by Emmair and Cadryn, Banprionsa was sure Tristan still felt responsible for her. His face now said more than any words. He had failed her.

"Cadryn, please tell me the boys are mistaken."

"No, her dragon says she can only feel her slightly. Something has definitely happened. We don't know what. Don't worry too much Tristan, we'll locate her."

As the two spoke, the Guardian strode over to where Banprionsa stood by herself, knowing she was like a mother bird who had lost her chick and wanted to fly off to rescue her.

When does your father arrive?

Ay d'noo ken. Soon, Ay would think.

Contact him for me. Ask how far away he is. I need his counsel.

Though the Guardian could have contacted Dubhbragh himself, he understood the need for Banprionsa to have something to keep her busy.

Banprionsa walked further from the rest of the group. Though dragons could hear what each other said at all times, they had learned to tune each other out so they would not listen in, like nosey crones.

Faither, where are ye?

What? Ay was taking a nap.

Ye were sleeping? Ay thought ye would be here any second.

Thare seemed little hurry. We saw this beautiful valley with luscious grass, deer and jackrabbits everywhere. We hunted and then stopped by the river to rest on the banks before we continued on our way.

Faither, ye need to come now. Really, right now.

Banprionsa, haes something happened? Are ye alright?

No, Ay am noo. Siona hae gone missing and naebody can locate her.

Now, d'noo overreact.

Ay is noo overreacting. Something is keeping me from Siona. Ay can only feel a shell of her soul.

Are ye saying she is dying?

Ay d'noo ken. Ye need to come right now.

Alright, let me gaither the others. We will be thare within the hour. Tell the Guardian. And stop worrying. Ay is sure she is fine.

Banprionsa returned to where the Guardian stood and repeated what her father had told her. As soon as she finished, he told her to go organize the dragons and have them and their talkers work together to see if there were any matches here. It was essential that they pick each other. If a rider and dragon didn't bond naturally, if forced together, many would take the path of wrong, as the connection was not true. Others took that path, as it was their natural inclination. Some, like Banprionsa's grandfather, took a wrong turn when offered wealth for loyalty. It was too late when he learned it wasn't worth it.

But Ay want to help find Siona. It is what Ay need to do.

Banprionsa, what we are doing right now you can't help with, said the Guardian.

But.

Can you climb the stairs, go into the dungeon, check the kitchen? No, you cannot. So I need you to do something else. Get the others ready. When Dubhbragh arrives, return to us.

Nodding, she walked over to the two dragons with their talkers. She noticed the small group of the two-footed. They were so alike in appearance: two arms, two legs, a hornless head, no tail. Mix them all together. It was like looking at a sea of wildflowers. Like wildflowers, some had characteristics that distinguished their variety. The taller willow-slender bunch had ears that stuck out like hot red peppers from the vine. Some were shorter, nearly as wide as tall, with bodies appearing carved from stone, their muscles not hidden by what they wore. Others were of middle build and rounded ears. These had the greatest variation in height. Here and there among the three races were a very few that looked like a mixture of two, as if someone had merged them like butter melted into bread. Banprionsa knew the races were more similar than they used to be. They spent so much time together that for some, only the outside features distinguished them from each other.

We are to gaither the others together and start the selection process. Ye boys, am sorry Ay d'noo remember yer names.

Ryuu.

Pogee.

Thank ye. Ay will try not to forget. Collect the rest of the Guides. We should begin with thaim. Meet hus back here.

As Ryuu and Pogee went to retrieve the Guides, Banprionsa turned to the two dragons.

Do ye remember how we hae been told the selection works? Tis much like a bird selecting its mate.

The young dragons continued to look bemused, so Banprionsa reminded them that when dragons first met humans, the Guardian had touched Dubhbragh's neck and his scales glowed, the blazing gold of starlight.

Do ye understand what needs to happen?

Banprionsa, that canna be right. It hasnae happened with either Gormcleite or myself, said Glascruba.

Glascruba is right. Our scales hinna glowed.

Hae ye offered yer neck for thaim to touch? The two looked slightly confused by this. *Try it when thay return and if Ay is right... Just do what Ay ask.*

When the boys returned with the Guides, the dragons spoke to their talkers. The moment Ryuu touched Glascruba, her scales bloomed the green of a Moray fish, her claws glowed like the forest leaves. Her claws radiated. While Ryuu touched Glascruba, Gormcleite watched and once she saw Glascruba glow, she lowered her head to Pogee. Pogee slowly reached over to touch Glascruba's feathers. As he made contact, it was if every cloud had left the sky. The blue of her feathers emitted a light that surrounded both of them like a halo. Nodding to Banprionsa, they explained to their talkers that each person would touch a dragon or dragons to see if they would bond with them. Before rejoining the adults, she had one last piece of information to impart.

Tell the two-footed races we are not all here, so not everyone's dragon will be here. If thay d'noo bond with someone, let thaim ken thare are more of hus comin and thay should have patience.

We hae a question. Why are these two-footed called the Guides? said Gearcleite.

Ryuu and Pogee looked at each other. Pogee took up the story.

I'll give you the short version. The castle itself is magic. In it, there are seven rooms for the original seven houses of the first guides. Each room has a piece of its makers-spirit that still lives there. This year during the festival the people toured the castle and the room choose who would live there. It marked them and it joined them to that room. Magically linked to its creator. That's why they call them the Guides.

So, the rooms chose thaim? said Gormcleite.

The two boys nod.

Then why are thare nine guides here and what are all the other two-footed doing here? said Gearcleite.

Oh, that's because some rooms took two people, like my twin brother and sister. The other was the warrior room. It took a boy and a girl. Not sure why it needed a girl.

Suddenly, Glascruba reached her tail around and tapped Ryuu none too gently on the head. *Watch it boy, YE BEST REMEMBER AY AM A GIRL!*

Yes, Glascruba.

The boys explained to the Guides how to greet the dragons, and they went to see the five dragons that were there. Quickly, three of the dragons glowed as the less apprehensive among the Guides had not hesitated in touching these magnificent beings.

The Guardian watched as Banprionsa returned to them.

Should not the brother of Siona be over with the others?

No, we need Tristan here. He is the one most likely to know all the places Siona would go to if she needed to hide.

Ay am sorry Tristan. Ay understand how ye are feeling.

Though Tristan did not know what she had said, he nodded at the Dragon. One look told him she was as worried as he was. Just a moment later, the sun darkened as if night had come: the adult dragons had arrived.

Dubhbragh told them they should land at the far end of the dragon alley, away from the two-footed and the young ones. Once all had gathered, they would move as a whole to greet the Guardian.

The Guardian and his small group strolled across dragon alley to a slight hill and there stopped and waited. Banprionsa could hardly stand even the most minor delay. She needed to find Siona, and all of this adult nonsense was killing her. She should just take off and start her own search.

Don't do it, Banprionsa. Came the twin voices of her father and the Guardian.

The dragons rocked forward, their tails swaying behind them, Dubhbragh in the lead. He started the formal greeting to the Guardian, who waved him off.

I think we may dispense with the niceties given the gravity of the situation. We are missing a talker. Someone has taken the girl.

One dragon stepped forward. *Why should one human child make a difference to us?*

Cadryn stepped forward, fury radiating out of him. He could not believe what he had just heard from Fadcruba, a voice he had not heard in so long, but would never forget. *YOU, Fadcruba, should care as she is my daughter and you know how much family means to me.*

Banprionsa stood still, stunned into silence. *Fadcruba could talk to a human. He had a dragon talker. But he had made so much fun of her. Why?*

For a moment, all they heard was the rustle of the wind through the grass. Fadcruba's scales turned turquoise in amazement. *Cadryn?*

Yes, and my Siona is missing. What do you say?

Well, what are ye waiting for? Let's go find the wee ane. Ay can hardly believe we get to meet. Cadryn, Ay have not haurd yer voice in my mind for many years. Ay hae missed being a part of ye.

Banprionsa saw Cadryn reached across and touched Fadcruba's neck, his scales illuminated as the dragon and talker met in person for the first time.

Wait, we need to be organized. Form a plan, Cadryn said.

But first you'd best call the young ones in now, said the Guardian.

Oracruba, stop hiding and come here, bring the others with ye. We hae need of ye, said Fadcruba.

A flock of dragons appeared over the horizon. The one in the lead was the color of sunshine dipped in the orange flame of evening.

Fadcruba turned furious as others commented on the beauty of his son. *He should noo be here; he's gaun to make a fool of himsel.*

As Oracruba landed, he didn't stumble, but hopped on the smooth grass, closing the distance between him and the others. Tristan could hardly believe what he saw: a dragon with a crippled leg. Oh, but so beautiful. He wanted to reach out and touch him.

Look, Ay d'noo fall. Ay like it here.

I am the Guardian and I welcome you to Ashwind Village, son of Fadcruba, and welcome all to of you. Normally we would have a celebration, but right now there is a problem and your help is required.

Banprionsa watched as the drama unfolded before her. She listened, both intrigued and inpatient at the same time.

While the Guardian talked, Tristan and Oracruba eyed each other. Tristan moved closer to the sun dragon. Cadryn noticed and moved over, too.

"Do you want to touch him?"

"Yes, I feel as if I know him, as if we are alike."

"Ask him. If he lowers his head, you may touch him. If not, you must wait."

Understanding what was being said, Oracruba lowered his head. Unlike the others, his scales became like sunshine itself, even before Tristan's hand made contact. Their link was strong.

It seems Fadcruba, that your son bonded with the leader of the Guides, said Cadryn.

No, that canna be. He is a crippled, and he is noo good enough for the leader of such a group.

Fadcruba, many think my son, Tristan, is not good enough to be the leader, as he is lame. Together, they can show the others that leading isn't all about being the most agile.

Bowing his head in acknowledgment and a certain shame, for the first time in years, Fadcruba knew pride in the child he had resented.

Banprionsa kept her eyes scanning and her ears tuned in to what was being said. As the adults talked, a small group moved towards them. She didn't know it was the FOP. She thought they wanted to get closer to the dragons.

Banprionsa was too far from the three that had come up. She watched, thinking they were trying to ask if they could meet the dragons. Banprionsa could barely hear what the three were saying. She had to tune into them and shut everything else out.

The three stood quietly and once they learned the search wasn't starting immediately, Carin, Nessa and the boy that they nicknamed the Mountain huddled together and formed a plan.

"It seems like Cadryn doesn't care much for his new daughter," said the Mountain.

"Now you know that's not true. You've seen the way he carries her on his shoulders whenever he gets a chance," said Nessa.

"I don't know, Nessa. You would have thought they would have sent someone after her by now," said Carin.

"And you know that whoever took her will hurt her," said the Mountain.

"Why do you say that? It can't be true. They just probably want something like food or money."

"Really Nessa, are you that naïve? You remember the girl from our village, don't you?" said Carin. "She was never the same after they found her."

Banprionsa shook her head. For a moment, hope had flowed into her, but quickly leeched away. The adults were already fast into their discussion. With her hearing, she could effortlessly understand what the three near her were saying. Would the person hurt her talker, her friend? She needed to go find Siona now. Careful to shield her thoughts, she quietly made her way to the tree line. She hopped along the tops of the evergreens and from there took off. If they would not look for Siona, she would.

7

Chapter 7 –The FOP

As the three watched Banprionsa slip away unnoticed, they too left Dragon Alley. Carin and Nessa left the Mountain behind to monitor things while they headed out of Ashwind City proper. They rapidly ducked into the woods and into a cave they used to contact the Old man. They went into a small cavern with water running down its walls. The ceiling was black with the soot of a thousand torches. Then Carin went to a small shelf recessed in the wall and pulled out a silver bowl. Nessa poured water into the vessel and waved her hand over it. She mumbled words she had memorized, but didn't understand. The place where the old man lived came into focus and they could see him securing the girl to a wall with chains.

"Sir, we have news," said Carin.

"Go on."

"The girl's dragon has left Dragon Alley to search for her talker."

"Good, good. Anything else?"

"Not yet."

"Let me know when they send out a search party when they are underway. Go, bond with a dragon. You might need their help."

With that, the old man waved his hand over the silver bowl at his side and he was gone. Carin dumped the water and hid the bowl. They then headed back to Dragon Alley. It wouldn't do either of them good if they didn't appear to be excited about the dragons. They wanted dragons, they just didn't want the half-breeds, dwarves and elves to have them. After all, they were inferior to humans and should be kept in their places. They and their friends needed to be among the first to touch the dragons. That way, they could be sure that their inferiors didn't bond with one.

8

Chapter 8 - Banprionsa's Search

Banprionsa found as she went west toward the ocean she could not feel Siona anymore, so she turned to the east and traveled for hours, knowing only that the connection was still there. No matter how slight the contact was now, she trusted it would become more distinct as she neared Siona.

She had flown for what seemed like forever and only now noticed the change in the land, that snow sprinkled the mountains like salt. That below to the south there was a desert with little water, that the valleys she crossed had strange flowers or that even deeper in the forest the elder trees tried to speak to her, warn her. She had shut her mind to little more than a spiral of a wave; hearing nothing, seeing nothing, but what was inside? Only the realization that she required food and water brought her out of it. She knew also that she needed to rest soon. Searching at night would not be fruitful. She needed her keen eyesight to watch for any signs.

Banprionsa worked her way out of the forest tops and into the valley. She made her way to the stream where the water was greener than the more familiar blue of the ocean. She bent her neck and took a delicate sip. It tasted like the evergreen leaves she loved so well. She downed her fill and turned to look for prey. Jackrabbit was her favorite; however, a chicken would do.

She was concentrating so much on the jackrabbit she spotted she did not notice the humans approaching. As she lowered her head, they flung a chain noose over it. Several adults heaved on the chain, which cut into her neck, slowing her breath, staunching her ability to breathe out flames. She struggled to free herself, but an old man with a white beard stepped in front of her. He stared deeply into her eyes, seized the horn on her brow, leaned in close, his sour breath assaulting her nose and muttered, *You will follow and not try to escape.*

Someone subjugated her will. They floated her deep into a cave hidden behind a towering waterfall. The noise was deafening, even for a dragon. As they moved into the second cavern, she couldn't believe it. She could feel Siona here. At the third cavern there she was, manacled to a wall. They placed Banprionsa next to her, chaining her so that the two could touch each other, but not much more. Banprionsa was relieved. It looked like Siona was in a deep sleep and nothing more.

The man with the white beard stopped in front of her. *If you try to escape, I will kill her. I know you understand me. I once talked to dragons all the time. We will speak later.*

***

Dubhbragh looked around and wondered where was Banprionsa. He couldn't believe she was not right here with them. He reached out to her. No answer was forthcoming. He called again, this time with impatience, telling her they would leave her if she did not come right now. Looking up, he let the Guardian know Banprionsa had gone. He looked the group over, knowing there would be many who would disagree with what he was going to suggest.

We need to call Galtenga, Banprionsa's biological grandfaither. Ay am not linked to her except by our great love. The ancient bloodlines link him. He will ken if she is hurt, or worse.

He's banished for a reason. We canna call him, said Fadcruba.

Aye, he made bad choices, and we decided noo to forgive him. Even after Banprionsa was born and her mither and faither died, we continued to punish him. Only letting him bury his dochter and bond with the wee ane so she would thrive.

The dragon council continued to argue against any communication with Banprionsa's grandfather. Then one of the council said that Galtenga had promised he would show how he had changed.

At this, the Guardian interrupted. *I know he is different now. Someone attacked the Lion Room using old magic.*

See, he's noo to be trusted.

You are wrong. He saved us from the creature. Saved our worlds from great devastation.

Voices raised as one, the Guardian and Dubhbragh commanded the quiet of all.

Will you believe the guide if I ask them to tell the story? The one who brought the room back to us. I will let you ask the questions and the dragon talkers will translate what you say, the Guardian said.

They dragged Pogee and Ryuu away from their new friends to join the adults. They grumbled all the way. Their father gave them a look that would have quelled a rabid dog, and they immediately ceased their complaining. He gave them instruction and told them not to add their own thoughts. Pogee nodded. He would start, while Ryuu went to get Brydon and Mirah. Once everyone was there, they asked the questions and the story unfolded.

9

Chapter 9—The Lion Room

They had taught the two children who had entered the Lion Room the old evils. They were excited. It was a chance for them to show their loyalty. It was up to them to destroy this room and keep the Guides from having a chance. Without a leader, the guides couldn't function.

They chanted the words used to kill a spirit. The Lion sprang from the door protecting its essence. It fought back, shooting magic from its eyes, using its tail to fend off the worse of the curses, but the Lion soon found he was fading. There were two of them and though he was strong, they had evil in their veins. They had taught the children the curses that nobody had uttered in generations. They flung them without remorse at the Lion.

The children only thought of the glory it would give them. How they could keep those of inferior races from rising above themselves. They knew the Guardian had asked for all to come to the festival. They knew the story of the rooms and how each had a piece of a spirit. That the rooms would choose even an inferior to live there if it wanted. This fueled their hate. They couldn't allow dwarf or elf or worse, a half-breed to live in the castle and reside in these rooms. The children had wanted to destroy all the spirits, but had ordered to only touch the Lion Room. The FOP thought that without a leader, the Guardian wouldn't have the rooms select anyone. That he would give up his notion of the Guides and realize that only purebred humans could rule and save them in the next war.

As the spirit of the Lion thought to give in, it heard the roar of an old friend, a dragon, Galtenga. Using the last of its strength, it spread the window wide, allowing the being to enter. The children had been unaware that the spirit of the Lion continued to be connected to the old dragon. That their friendship and love transcended even the death of his mate. Some believed that the rooms held only the spirit of the maker. They didn't know or had forgotten that the makers each had a dragon they bonded to and the dragon, too, had lent some of its spirit to the room.

The dragon lashed its tail at the children, disrupting their chant. Urging the Lion to go under, it held the children back. This gave the Lion a chance to take its spirit deep into Mother Earth to heal. It watched from its hiding place as its old friend fought this new foe. The dragon snarled and spit fire. It reached out to hurt or kill, fighting the instinct to protect children. Maybe this caused it to not go as harshly as it could have. The children were quick to bring up a shield and scream curses that just bounced off of the old dragon, embedding the curses instead in the wall, causing the room to groan in pain.

The children knew the dragon was stronger than they and took off down the stairs and slammed out of the Castle. They dashed into the woods and fled east toward their village. The dragon followed, shooting fire at them, careful to not start his forest home on fire. Once he was sure that the children were gone, he circled back to the room.

He squeezed back through the window and tried to bring the Lion back from the earth. He used all the magic in him to call forth the spirit that he loved. It was not enough; the Lion was half dead and he could not reach it. All he might do was cry his dragon tears into where he thought it had gone, hoping their healing powers could penetrate and help the Lion return to its place.

Do ye now recognize who that is, from what the boy has said? Is that noo enough for ye? We are noo asking him to rejoin hus, only allow him to help in search of the granddaughter that daesna ken him, said Dubhbragh. *Thare is mare to the story if ye need it.*

Most dragons agreed it was enough they could contact him.

Whit of the wizard, daes he live? said Fadcruba.

Yes, said the Guardian.

Have ye contact? asked Fadcruba.

No, just knowledge. Just as you banished Galtenga, we banished him. It was the way.

There were some who still continued the argument until Cadryn could stand it no more. *If Galtenga can help us find Banprionsa and she can help find Siona, then the decision is made. Our children are more important than an age-old banishment.*

Ye d'noo understand, said Fadcruba.

You are right, I don't, and I don't even want to. All I want is the children back.

How do we even ken that Galtenga will help? asked Fadcruba.

And miss a chance to meet the granddaughter we hae denied him? Really? said Dubhbragh.

The Guardian and Dubhbragh looked at each other. They knew that one of them could open the ancient link, rusty as it was, and ask them to come. They decided it would be best to try the dragon link. Dubhbragh moved away from the crowds and faced the mountains. He noticed the trees were two times taller than when he had last been here. He saw the Guardian had kept his word and the trail to the Dragon Caves was still clear. His eyes wandered to the topmost peak where the snow encircled it like a crown. Yes, there was the old eagle's nest and just coming in from the south, he could see a convocation of eagles. Once he would have flown to greet them and ask if they had news, but eagles did not live as long as dragons. It would take time, but they could form new friendships with old allies.

He knew he was stalling. It was time to reach out to Galtenga. In the younger days, they had been inseparable, their colors complementing each other. When battles had come, they knew what the other would do. They had formed a powerful force for their side, until they had swayed Galtenga, mesmerized by the promise of power that would never, could never have been his. Then they found themselves on opposite sides of the battle. His only failure was to not have killed him. Something he never regretted. He knew his friend still lived behind the mask that he wore. Shaking his head, he concentrated his every thought into a single conduit. He knew he would only have this one chance, and he needed to do it right. He forced every other thought from his head.

Galtenga, Ay need to speik to ye, auld friend.

No response.

This is important, ye son of a horse.

Still nothing more than a small tingle.

My dochter nay, your granddaughter is amiss, and Ay fear for her.

Whit did ye call me? How dare ye use Banprionsa to get me to answer ye? Ay hae tried to contact ye and n'er once did ye answer.

The council forbid it, ye ken that.

Ye head the council. Ye could hae.

Stop, bring the wizard and come to dragon alley. Yer granddaughter and her talker are missing.

MY GRANDDAUGHTER HAS A TALKER?

Will ye just come? Ay will explain everything. Ay give ye my oath that naebody shall harm ye or that damnable wizard of yers.

Where?

Ashwind Village, behind the castle. Ay understand ye have been here before.

We will be thare in the morning. Ay need to prepare.

Slowly, with his head down, he rejoined the group.

He will come here at first light. Now we should organize the wee anes so thay can begin thair training. Ay do noo think thare is time to waste. Ay fear something bigger is gaun on.

10

Chapter 10 - The Joining

Tristan and Oracruba walked over to where the two boys had given up. Mayhem was all that was going on. All five of the original dragons had bonded with the two-footed. The others who had just wandered over only saw that there were not enough two-footed for all of them. They were arguing over who the two-footed should talk to first.

The Guides sat back and stared at the giant-sized children as smoke, fire and spit-stream came out of their noses and mouths. They stayed back as the spit could melt rock — as it had done that to a stone they had been throwing around earlier that day. As Tristan and Oracruba walked up, quiet descended upon the group. Ryuu and Pogee shrugged their small shoulders as if to say *what did you expect* and rejoined their dragons. Tristan weighed into the mix, Oracruba by his side. He waved for Pogee and Ryuu to rejoin him. He told them he needed them to translate. Then he gave his instruction.

"All right, if you have bonded, move over there," he said, pointing to the blue-gray wall that surrounded the castle. "If you have not, line up behind me."

As soon as both children and dragons started for him, Tristan realized his mistake.

He held up his hand, and everyone stopped moving.

"Stop! Students, line-up behind me."

Looking up at those who still stood at the ramparts, he told them if they wanted a chance to be a rider; they needed to get down here now. One girl started climbing down the vine on the castle walls.

"Not a good idea. If you break your leg, you won't have time to meet them. Go the long way."

Soon, the line extended over the small hill, almost to the end of Dragon Alley. Not just students were there, but apprentices and shop-keepers' children. Tristan decided everyone should go through and hopefully each dragon would find a rider. They started with adults who could ride a horse. It would give them a chance to see if they could bond with one of the older dragons. If not all dragons bonded, then the others adults would have a chance.

Some didn't join the line. There was one girl, Tegan, who watched with envy. She wanted nothing more than to touch these magnificent beings. As she looked, she noticed not all the dragons were the same. There were, in fact, four different races. They looked like they could be four opposing armies.

There was one that instead of wings had two ridges of rear curving scales the size of large baker's paddles used to get bread out of the oven. She wondered what they were for. Then, there was an enormous dragon with wings like old leather that looked like giant bat wings. Next, there was a smaller size dragon with shorter front legs and rear legs that reminded her of a grasshopper made for jumping. Their wings were short but ran the length of their body, almost like twin fins. Last was the one she wished she could touch; it had feather-like scales. Its wings were long like a gull's, but wonderfully colored and, to her mind, more beautiful than a butterfly.

Tegan knew that the old man, her grandfather, wouldn't be pleased if she bonded without talking to him. She decided she would try to discuss it with him. But he had clarified that he didn't like or trust the Guardian. He only allowed her to go to the castle to gather information. She didn't understand. Everyone here seemed nice and the children who went to school here appeared to like it. She loved learning and wished that she too went to the school.

The heat of the day was long past, and the sun was saying goodnight to the moon when the last dragon and rider of the day were paired. Training would begin tomorrow. Tonight was a time for rest and to send prayers to Mother Earth that their girls hadn't been harmed.

There was one last surprise that day. As Emmair stood next to her husband and Fadcruba, a dragon walked over and stood close to her. This one felt different, friendlier, like it was more of a sparrow than a hawk. The Guardian, seeing this from the corner of his eye and knowing that Emmair was not used to these beings, walked over and introduced himself to the newcomer. The dragon was of middle years and had not yet found its rider. She told the Guardian that she would like the watcher of children to touch her. She too watched the children, and she thought they belonged together. Bonded, they could keep the children safer than either of them had separately. She blamed herself for the young dragons' flight to Ashwind and knew without words that Emmair blamed herself for the two that were missing, even if one was a dragon. The Guardian translated this to Emmair, who gaped.

With a little urging, she reached with a pale and trembling hand and touched Imfiac's scales. They glowed like buttercups in the sunlight. Scared, but pleased, she continued to caress the dragon, and a bond was born between the caretakers of the young.

11

Chapter 11—The Exiles Return

Galtenga traipsed in front of the cave, impatient that the old wizard wasn't ready. He needed to get to Ashwind City to find the granddaughter denied him for the sins of his youth. He and his rider had made bad choices. The promise of gold had lured them to the side of their enemies. Instead of gold, they ended up living in a dank cave above a humble village, hiding from all. He could only fly when the sky was sightless. But no more. Today he would fly to Ashwind and show them he belonged with his kind. He was older and longed for the company of other dragons. The wizard came out, and Galtenga lowered himself to let the old man climb on his back.

They took to the air. No circuitous route this time. He flew straight over the village with its thatched roof houses and neatly planted crops. The first travelers were on the road and he dipped a wing to them. He sailed over the golden wheat plains where groups of farmers worked to gather the crops. Past the tops of the old trees, so dense you could not see the ground. The small strip of desert that came next was barren except for the Joshua trees that loved the dry heat.

The two spoke of old friends from their youth and of what brought them to this point. They hoped that calling for them meant old wounds would be forgiven. As they reminisced, they went back hundreds of years to their youth when they played as much as they trained. Until that day, when they headed out for adventure and found more...

Freedom for three whole days. They had been training non-stop for weeks, and now they had a chance just to explore. Dubhbragh, Galtenga and Luchcruba left the dragon hold and were heading to Castle Farraige to join their riders. The sun hadn't even tipped the horizon, and the moon had only just fallen asleep as it ducked behind the castle parapet. Still enough light to show their way. They glided on the winds and dipped their wings into the sea, leaving trails of glowing white foam. Luchcruba immersed his wing farther, came up and flung water, spraying the other two as he soared above them. Puffs of smoke shot from their nostrils as they engorged their wings to reach him. Luchcruba had timed his attack perfectly. As they rounded the curve, there were their riders. They lined up in a "V" formation and headed in, landing smoothly; they touched down at the same time. Their riders ambled toward them, carrying sacks with food and ragged blankets for sleeping. They were heading out for three days of exploration. They wanted to see the inner reaches of their lands, to go where few had ventured.

The Guardian clambered onto Dubhbragh. "Little brother, it's time, so stop stalling."

"Yeah, yeah!" said Garvin.

The Guardian turned, intently studying the wizard. "Conall, come on, you can practice your magic later. Let's go."

At that, a ball of fire headed his way and exploded into stars, just as the other two burst into laughter. Groaning, he signaled to Dubhbragh to take off, as he tried to keep his bubbling laughter from escaping.

They soared at different heights. The land here was familiar. They could see the fields of gold below, and the mountains with tips of white in the far distance. Those ice-clad heights were their ultimate destination. Galtenga was hungry, and he glided among the redwoods watching for a random rabbit. There, he saw three and signaled to his rider, the wizard. Diving, he swooped close to the ground and noticed that the rabbits stopped and wheeled, as they recognized a predator. They took off, and he chased them for about a quarter of a mile, flying close to the ground. Using his leather-like wings, he herded them away from the woods. He dodged over rocks and under low-hanging branches, Conall leaning far over his neck, stretching forward as if he slept, so he and his dragon melded, indistinguishable. Dubhbragh let him know he could see their warren coming up. With a powerful down thrust of his wings, he shot ahead, snagging the three rabbits in his talons. They squirmed in his grasp. He wanted to keep them alive until they stopped for breakfast. Rabbit tasted better if they were fresh. He almost dropped one as it wiggled for its freedom.

Luchcruba spotted a meadow near a gurgling stream they had often visited before, signaled that they should stop. Galtenga let the other two land, then he tossed the struggling rabbits to them as he floated down. He landed right at the bank of the stream.

As they had often camped before, they knew each other's strengths. So, they went to their usual tasks. The Wizard gathered wood. While the Guardian went for water, Garvin would make the meal. Though all three could cook, he had a way with herbs, mixing and matching so that even the old tough jack-rabbits would taste like the choicest meat. He retrieved his cutting board and knife, then with a flick of his wand, the blade chopped the onion and garlic on its own, as if a whirlwind had held the knife in its grasp. While the knife performed the cutting, Garvin clutched each squirming rabbit. With a quick twist of his wrist, the wriggling stopped. Shortly, on the wind came the smell of sizzling flesh, garlic and onion. The saliva-inducing scents permeated the air, causing their six stomachs to rumble in concert. They all sat by the smoldering fire and watched the day be born. The sky filled with gold, reflecting off the poppies of the fields.

The old wizard smiled as he remembered the time spent with the two who were brothers and as close to him as if he, too, were their blood. He reminded Galtenga of the trick that only Garvin could do. Garvin, the youngest, whose nickname was *the old man*. Which still seemed funny to him, as the Guardian acted more like an old man. Galtenga went on about the trick Garvin, the old man, had played on Dubhbragh that day.

While they were repacking their belongings, Garvin shouted to the others to watch him as he levitated a large log. The Guardian laughingly yelled to his brother, "That would be impressive if you could do that with Dubhbragh."

Before he could draw breath, Dubhbragh was floating in the air, legs pin-wheeling, searching for purchase, scales strobing a surprised turquoise. With a flick of his wand, Garvin flipped him on his back, twisted him to the right, then to the left, tossing him as if Dubhbragh was as light as a new babe. The dragon, scales burning dark blue with frustration, could not free himself. His colors strobed from blue to orange as his frustration grew to anger, as the others' laughter rose around him.

The Wizard snickered. "Can you show me that trick?"

"No."

Garvin, none too gently, dropped Dubhbragh, then bounded onto Luchcruba's back and took to the air. He knew he needed to move fast as a gyrfalcon until Dubhbragh calmed down.

The three dragons felt the intense exaltation of expanding their wings in flight. By directing blood through hollow bones to reach the tips, they gained extra length they did not need on the ground. They wheeled and dove through clouds and changed them to shapes of birds, trees or animals, dragon art. They flew for the next few hours, still soaring through familiar lands. As they reached the limit of where they had ventured before, each made a loop and plunged toward the ground to see who would fall closest to disaster before pulling up.

Laughter and smoke filled the air as the six soared on with no thoughts of the future.

They sped onward until day's end as the world gradually shifted from the greens of the meadows to brown hard-packed earth. The lack of rain cracked the land and they could see only scraggly Joshua trees that provided no shade. Branches like dried balls flowed across the open spaces, moved by the fancy of the wind. The Wizard snagged one and found it had sharp points like rose stems; he quickly let go as an orb of blood welled from his finger.

The sun was dipping behind the mountains as the friends stopped for the night. They cautiously gathered the weeds that peppered the plains and made a fire, bringing out rations from the bags they carried. The wind picked up, and the temperature went from mild to icy as the moon greeted the purple sky. The mountains looked like periwinkle dots in the hazy distance, and they knew they could not make it there in the time remaining. Besides, the dragons could see the ancient forest a few miles off, felt them as if they were being summoned. They would leave the mountains for another day and head toward the old woods.

At the birth of the new day, the visceral feeling of being pulled toward the forest spread rapidly through the three dragons. They shared this feeling with their riders and they set off immediately. Before the sun had fully risen, they had reached the outskirts of the woods. A voice, like a siren's song, whispered in their minds urging them to fly further into the woods, gently directing them deep into its cloak of mist, until it accompanied them down through a funnel of trees and into a large amphitheater with a stone altar at one end. Elves had covered the altar in runes and the wizard strode over to examine them.

Before he could reach the step, the wind knocked him back, as if a hand shoved at his chest. The voice they heard came on the wind. "Hold a moment. This is not your place; first we must speak. Dragons helped shape these woods. They once played in our creeks and dales. You were our most trusted ally, and it has been ages since you scattered in the wind," said the voice of the trees. "We have never understood why you abandoned us for the two-footed races. Or why you didn't bring them to us?"

We hae haurd legends of the elders of the woods. Ay see now thair truth, Dubhbragh said while the others stood like statues.

"It didn't surprise us when we became just stories for the two-footed races, but we had expected more of you dragons."

"Wait a minute..." said Garvin.

"Perhaps it would be a good time for you to speak less and listen more," said the ancient trees.

Thare's an idea worth heeding, said Dubhbragh. *Now, where were we?*

For hours, they spoke and shared stories of their histories and ways of life. The tree told of how the elves had moved in and lived with them in harmony. They had built the altar and would come when the new and old moon shone together in the sky. But, for the elder ones, losing the dragons had been traumatic. The elder spoke of a war that would come before the next moon and that old friends would turn on each other in search of an alternative path. She could not see the outcome. A veil obscured this part of the coming battles. She wished them smooth winds and long updrafts as they parted. The dragons vowed they would share this meeting and return soon.

The dragons could smell the salt on the breeze miles before the humans could see the ocean. As they reached the coastline, they saw cliffs where the waves pounded faces into the rock. Further down the shore, they saw them, the Others. They had only heard about the strange beings who were as tall as the trees. Dragons of unknown silhouettes orbited in the air. They were heading toward Castle Farraige. Quickly, the compatriots circled, deciding to head inland slightly, to skirt the Others. They needed to return and warn the council. Garvin and the Wizard argued with the Guardian. They wanted to separate and see if they could talk to them, while the Guardian went and warned the council. But the Guardian wouldn't listen. He shooed them towards home and to the elders' council.

The two discussed how this had been when the split started. They went more out of pique. They had felt that their ideas were being ignored, and it opened the door for them to be lured to the other side. It was too late when they realized their mistake.

***

They were now back in the forest and there, there was Ashwind Village. Galtenga could see the large field area that was empty this early except for Dubhbragh and the Guardian. He landed and advanced quickly.

What news do ye hae? said Galtenga, his scales turning an anxious indigo. Under dragon law, when both parents have died, the grandparents become their legal parents. So, Banprionsa would call Galtenga Grandfather.

Hello old freend, we hae no news of Banprionsa and her talker. Hae ye tried the parent connection? Can ye feel her? said Dubhbragh.

Aye. She is alive, but noo free.

As the two dragons spoke to each other, the Guardian and the Wizard looked each other over. Once as close as brothers, then on opposite sides of a war. They knew more about each other than any, except their dragons. The Guardian accepted it was time to heal old wounds. Reaching out, he embraced his old friend.

"Welcome to Ashwind Village, Conall. It is time we forget past wrongs. We have work to do if you will join us."

Embracing his friend, Conall's voice constricted as he said, "I will."

It didn't surprise Galtenga to see others showing up directly after they greeted the Guardian. It surprised him what happened with the guides and how the boy Tristan took charge.

Others had been watching from out of sight, and soon there was a large group gathered around. The first order of business was who would look for the girls. Of course, Galtenga would lead the way; he had the strongest connection. Dubhbragh wanted to go, but they decided someone had to start the training the riders. Tristan too would go; it was his sister. He and Oracruba had practiced late into the night and when they said he couldn't go because he didn't know how to ride. Tristan showed them how wrong they were. Farah came riding in on Clochfiac saying they were going too. Several of the other Guides had practiced and stated their intention of going when Tristan put up his hand and quiet descended.

"Farah, you need to stay here, help the others. Dalton will be in charge while I'm gone. I need all of you to work with the rooms to look for the girls."

Then Tristan walked over to the adults and turned toward Conall. "Sir, we don't know you. So, besides you going, I would request that either Ferris or Ainmire come with us, too."

"I believe Ferris would agree that it should be me. I've been wandering the woods and speaking to the old trees. Banríoncruba and I practiced together, too," said Ainmire.

"I haven't bonded yet. Though I know more dragons come this morning. I think I should stay and help with the training," said Ferris, looking slightly relieved. "I can also see to equipment being made that will fit the various riders. You all will have to go without. Unless we can find something that will work."

"Guardian, do we have your permission to proceed? I need to go find my sister," said Tristan.

"Yes, Tristan, once again, I think you have the right of it. Just remember that Ainmire is in charge. You are to check in every few hours. Now let's head to the caves and see if any of the equipment there will work. I want you out before the first light fades."

12

Chapter 12 - Flight

Nobody noticed the old woman walking around giving out bread to the youngsters. If they had paid attention, they would have seen the bright, clear eyes shining out of an old weathered face. They would have noticed how close she came to the ones discussing the rescue. But the children, adults and dragons were all too busy learning about each other to notice one old woman. The ones making plans were too engrossed to notice anything. Once she knew their strategies, she limped unobserved beyond the castle wall. She shed her gray cloak, revealing a girl on the edge of womanhood. Tegan straighten her back, took off her wig, her blond hair tumbled to her waist. Her blues sparkling with determination, she whistled and a black horse, speckled in white as if drops of rain had bleached it, trotted up and stopped before her.

She vaulted into the saddle and headed east. Tegan needed to get to her grandfather and tell him what was going on. He needed to be prepared for those who searched for the girl and the dragon. Though she didn't understand why he captured them, her love for the old man had her racing back to him. Tegan knew she would have to race the wind to beat the dragons. Her only advantage was that she knew where the captives were and didn't need to search. As she plunged on, nature itself turned against her. Tree branches fell in her way, making her horse rear and, more than once, she lost her seat, landing on her rump until it was the color of a blueberry. She got to a small stream that she should have easily crossed when she heard a roar like an avalanche and water came pouring over her. Only her experience kept her from tumbling into the stream as it carried her and her mount downstream for several miles. When she finally could make her way across, she had lost much time. Tegan only took a moment to make sure the saddle was secure, and off she went.

As she arrived at the entrance of the cave, Tegan saw that the old man stood on the path leading to the waterfall and the cave entrance. His eyes raked the skyline as he shook his head with impatience. His granddaughter was late, and that was rare for her. The old man wanted Tegan safely with him. He worried every time she went to Ashwind Castle. Would the Guardian recognize her? Tegan looked so much like their mother and sister he couldn't see how the Guardian wouldn't notice they were family. The old man's wrinkled face was further furrowed by worry. He wondered where his granddaughter could be. She should have returned from Ashwind Village two hours ago. He looked off into the distance and saw the dust from a horse galloping toward him. He smiled as he scanned the horizon and saw none of his enemies.

Soon the girl had joined him, and they speedily went behind the veil of the falls. He beckoned her to sit, and she gravely told him all she had learned. Letting him know that the fathers of the girls were on the search. He should easily be able to defeat the small party. The old man wasn't worried about his captives. He was sure they were secure and could not run away. Between the chains and the magic, there wasn't much chance of that.

"Grandfather, if you have people in Ashwind, why do I need to go there at all?"

"Because you are the only one I truly trust. Are you worried that someone will find you out?"

"No, I just wondered. Should I head back soon?"

"Yes, that might be best. Just stay away from the one they call the Guardian."

"I will."

"Good."

"Grandfather, there is the most beautiful dragon. It is like she is calling to me."

"Stay away from the dragons." The old man jumped to his feet. "Don't touch them. Don't even think about it."

"But..."

"You will do as I say." He paced rapidly about the outer chamber. "If you touch the dragon and it glows, you are bound to it for life. I don't want that for you. It will tie you to the castle and to him, not me. Stay away."

Tegan didn't answer him; she bent her head and tried to hide the tears that came to her eyes. Tegan wanted this more than anything. She rarely asked for something for herself, and it hurt. Why couldn't or wouldn't he see how much it meant to her? She knew long ago he had been a dragon rider. That he had known the thrill and joy of being able to soar with the eagles. She didn't understand why he would deny her the same experiences.

The old man worried that the lure of the dragons would be too much; he couldn't let her fall into that trap. He hoped Tegan would heed his words. If not, he wasn't sure what he might do.

He watched Tegan ride until she was out of sight, then he turned and headed into the cave to check on his two captives.

***

Banprionsa and Siona were awake and alone. They took in the surroundings of the dank cave. Its only light was a little starlight that filtered through the caves' crevices. The cavern was in perpetual night and they did not know how long they had been there. The old man had kept them in a magical sleep so that this was the first they had awoken together. They noticed stalagmites grew in the middle of the cavern, away from where they were. It looked like shark teeth. They could see a fire burning and a blackened pot hung over it. A vile smell oozed out of it, reminding Siona of gathering dung for the garden. She hoped it wasn't dinner. The girls silently communicated their concerns and Banprionsa tried to contact her father. They feigned sleep and confusion. Each tested their bonds and found them to be solid. They discovered that Banprionsa's sharp claws could reach the bolts in the wall where Siona was tied. They concluded that each time Banprionsa was awake, and the man with the white beard gone, she would work on it like a mouse, a bite at a time so that nobody would notice. It was up to them to escape. Their families did not know where they were or how to find them.

The old man entered the cavern. There was a sack filled with vegetables, spices and a rabbit. He set the bag down and whistled as he got out a hatchet and a small knife. The old man opened the bag and pulled the squirming rabbit out. He laid his forearm along its body and though the rabbit's head moved; he slammed the hatched through the neck; the body twitched once, twice and then stopped.

From the corner of the cave, he heard Siona say, "Ew," while the dragon inhaled the smell of a fresh kill. Both reactions held the familiarity of old times. He looked over at the two, held the rabbit up and said, "Dinner." Without waiting for a response, he completed the skinning, put the meat into a pot to cook and hung the skin over the fire to dry out. He would add it to the pile he already had in the corner to make a blanket for winter. The blood that he had drained, he dumped into the pot that endlessly simmered over the coals. Though the girls didn't realize it, he was careful what he added to the brew. It would be the start of great magic, one he hoped would help him destroy the dragons.

13

Chapter 13—The Choice

Dalton surveyed the chaos going on and went to find the Guardian. He had an idea, but it would require his and Emmair's cooperation.

"Excuse me, could I talk? I have an idea and would like to talk it with you."

"What is it, Dalton?"

"It might be best if the mum of Brydon hears this, too."

The Guardian waved to Emmair, who walked over, bringing her dragon with her.

"Dalton would like to share an idea with us."

Emmair smiled at the boy, knowing he was the shyest of the guides and that he missed words.

"I think training with dragons start."

"Agreed. Let's hear your idea," said the Guardian.

"I think you train guides and some others, maybe the elf girl," said Dalton, pointing to Aine, "and warrior's cousin. Not just guides. You pick those learn the quickest."

"Sound idea. But what of the others?"

Dalton looked at Emmair and then down at the ground. "We need the little boys to help. They talk with the dragons and nobody else does as well as them."

"I'm not sure that's a good idea. Look what they're doing now. It's like they're trying to get on top of them."

"Yes, exactly what they are doing. If they helped, the Guardian give special riding lesson. They earn it. Like a job."

"I was thinking they would need a lesson soon, anyway. Or they would hurt themselves. Emmair, what do you say?" said the Guardian.

Emmair stood for a moment watching her sons, trying to scale the dragons they were bonded to. "Better you teach them the right way than they do it on their own. Only though if they do a good job helping. Now, how should the others be split?"

"Go on Dalton, tell us the rest of your idea."

"Brydon's Pa, should work to find the correct match. Then adults and children two groups. The dwarf teacher should be with the boy who is with kids. Different teacher with the adults. I don't know who. They should choose boy they can work with the best."

"Solid plan Dalton, go find Ferris and will see what teacher he thinks," said the Guardian.

Dalton hurried away and was soon back with Ferris, who was told the plan. He recommended they use Regan, who seemed unafraid of the dragons. Regan joined them and between them, they decided Pogee should work with Ferris and train the children. While Ryuu would work with Regan. Dalton went and got the boys, who were unhappy about being separated from their dragons.

When they were all together, Dalton explained that if the boys helped with training the others to speak with their dragons, they would get a special flying lesson.

"Boys, if you do a good job, the Guardian will give you a flying lesson today," said Emmair.

"We can fly today?" said Ryuu.

"Are you just making that up?" said Pogee.

"The only way you'll find out is to do what you're asked," said Emmair.

Dalton did what he thought Tristan would have done. He wandered among the groups, making sure that everyone had what they needed. Dalton murmured to a couple of adults that they needed to listen to Ryuu. Ryuu was only one of a handful of people who could communicate with the dragons. They would need to talk with their dragon before they could fly.

Emmair dragged the boys home for lunch after the morning training. The Guardian had agreed to give them a flying lesson after they had eaten and taken a break. They didn't want to wait, but one look from Dalton stopped them short.

Dalton saw the look of surprise on Pogee and Ryuu faces when they came back from lunch and saw a large group had gathered. Some to cheer them on, others in hopes they would fail. They were just children and many of the older youths and adults thought it should be them, not these two. Among the crowd who didn't want them to succeed was the old woman. Tegan's disguise once more was in place. She watched everything while sitting on one side of a grassy hump amidst the villagers. Nobody realized that none of them knew her.

Tegan sat there and watched the two young boys learn to fly. She joined in the laughter as they repeatedly tried to mount their dragons. She knew from learning to mount a horse that they would have bruises on their backsides as large as a frying pan. But now, both boys had done it a dozen times each, and they were going to get to fly. The Guardian had warned them not to go over two feet off the ground. More than that and they would be grounded for a week, literally. The dragons took off, and the boys glided across the field. They went three times around, shouting with glee and sounding like the geese when they were attacking their food. As they came around for the third time, the Guardian signaled them to land. As the dragons came to a halt, the boys tumbled off the front, with no more grace than a rock coming down the mountain. The crowd roared with laughter.

"That's enough for today, boys. Don't try this when I'm not around. I'll know if you do and you won't like what will happen if you ignore me."

At that pronouncement, the Guardian went to meet the new riders and see how Cadryn was doing, finding riders for those dragons who hadn't found one.

Tegan was jealous. To ride a dragon like those boys and her grandfather had been a dream she had shared with no one until yesterday. Then her grandfather had forbidden her. Didn't he understand if she bonded with one of them, she could come back as herself and train with them? Then she would know everything and not have to hide her identity. She would speak to him again and convince him.

Tegan looked over at the dragons; there were only a few remaining. If she wanted this, she would have to do it now. She could feel the pull, and it was too hard to resist. She should wait, talk to him once more. Abruptly, she changed her mind. No, she would just do it and then tell him. He would just have to understand.

As soon as those thoughts came into her, she took off around the corner of the castle. She found a place behind an old oak tree that had a hollow in the trunk. It was just her size. Tegan ducked in and took off the disguise, shaking out her long mane of blond hair. She quickly braided it and turned it into a topknot. She rolled down her pant legs and headed back in, wondering how to approach the dragons.

When she came back around, she saw a short line of people who were wandering among them. Some avoided touching any of them as if afraid they were on fire and any contact would burn. Others caressed them as if they were pet cats. At this, some dragons looked annoyed. She waited her turn, hoping that there would be at least one left. Tegan saw the one she had felt drawn to was still there. She held her breath, waiting, hoping until finally it was her turn. There were still four dragons left who hadn't bonded with anyone. Tegan didn't even think about it; she walked straight up to one that reminded her of the leaves as they floated to the ground, almost the color of a pumpkin, its wings highlighted with indigo stripes. She walked up, stopped and, as she heard others do, Teagan asked if she might touch him. He lowered his head and, as her hand made contact, his apricot scales radiated the vermillion of embers of a dying fire. She shivered and knew it was meant to be. Now she just had to tell her grandfather what she had done. But before she did that, she would need to speak with the enemy.

Tegan deliberately waylaid the Guardian when he had separated himself from the group of adults.

"Sir, I have to tell my family what has happened. It is too late to start today. May I sleep in the stables and go home tomorrow? I will come back the next day."

"Would you like me to contact them? I can do so through the fire and you would not have to make the trip. Many of the others will stay here. We think it best that all of you should remain at the castle and attend school, as well as work with the dragons."

No longer able to hold his glance, Tegan's eyes darted from the blue of the castle's parapets to the snow crowning the mountains. Her fawn brown eyes reflecting the unease she was trying to hide.

"No, they would not like a stranger to contact them. I will ask and let you know tomorrow. I help with chores and the garden. How often could I go home?"

As the Guardian watched her, he noticed the way her mouth turned down as she tried to hide the uneasiness, so familiar, he just couldn't place where. "If you chose, you could go home each Friday after dragon training and return Sunday evening before lights out, or with special permission, Monday morning before class."

Tegan breathed deeply, head bowed, so the relief she felt wouldn't show. She hurried to stable her horse. So she would be ready to leave early the next day to see her grandfather and tell him what she had done. Tegan wasn't sure of the reception she would receive. This was the first time she had disobeyed.

14

Chapter 14—The Searchers

Tegan knew the rescue party was well underway. She had overheard that they knew to go east, as Galtenga had come from the west and had felt only an echo of his daughter. The bond between parent and child in the dragon world was strengthened by magic within the first month of the child's birth. Galtenga attended the ceremony and his wife's burial. That was the last time he had seen Banprionsa. That did not make the bond any less reliable. The only thing that could change it was the death of either, or when the bond passed from parent to spouse. The six carefully searched each square mile. They went low into valleys and saw the last of the sunflower-yellow primroses blooming on the banks of the brooks.

They frightened the outlying town's people, who had not heard the news that dragons actually exist. Children ran after them in awe, waving at them as if a storybook had come to life. The youngsters wanted to get closer, to touch them, to feel their scales or feathers. They saw the beauty of the enormous flying creatures and wanted to join those that were riding them. The adults did not feel the same way. Some of them took aim with crossbows and tried to shoot the fliers down. They feared the stories they had heard of dragons during the old war who had burned towns, villages, houses, crops to dust. They didn't want that nightmare to become their life. The searchers had to be careful, but they continued.

Every mile or so Galtenga called to Banprionsa, reaching his thoughts as far as he could stretch them. Like a spring, it snapped back and hit him. There was no answer. Mile after mile, they flew.

Tristan finally signaled that he wanted to land. He needed a drink and food. He was also getting sore as he had never ridden a dragon before last evening and it had been a long time since he had ridden even a donkey. Though this was serious business, he could not overcome the joy he felt in flying. He tried hard to communicate with Oracruba and had some success once the Wizard gave him some help. He learned he needed to think in pictures and to open his mind to allow Oracruba to send pictures to him. Tristan had learned that Fadcruba hadn't been happy to have a son who was lame. That he hadn't seen how the others came to him for advice. Fadcruba had only seen the outside. Oracruba still hoped he could show his father that he had value.

After they landed and had rested, Oracruba wandered downstream. He called the others over and showed them what he had found: dragon tracks. They could only be from Banprionsa, as no other dragons would have been this way. They could see marks of chains being dragged on the ground and, after a moment, no tracks. The Wizard closed his eyes and imaged what had happened here. He saw it all clearly. He and the Guardian only knew of one person with that kind of magic. But that couldn't be. The man was dead. He had to be sure before he told the Guardian. The Wizard had caused so much hurt already. If he could spare the Guardian this, he would.

Do you think we should tell the Guardian that someone is levitating dragons? said Galtenga.

We have only known one person to have mastered that. I wish to be sure before I tell him his brother might be alive; said The Wizard.

Galtenga reached out to Dubhbragh and the Guardian. He closed his eyes before he told them they had found signs that Banprionsa had come this way. In the end, they decided that the six of them would continue the search.

In the morning, Tristan watched as Galtenga and Conall walked over to the area where Banprionsa's tracks were. The Wizard muttered to himself the entire time, while Galtenga tried to see where the drag marks of the chain went. The only problem was, they disappeared at the edge of the stream. No matter where on the opposite side they looked, the only thing that they could see were prints of old sandals worn down with time. The spongy moss held the prints as if they had left behind the shoes. It showed exactly where the big toe had broken through the sole of the sandal. Of Banprionsa, there was no trace.

They rejoined the others, shaking their heads. The six conversed for a while before Conall spoke, telling them he knew of only one way this could have happened. Someone had levitated the dragon, moving her above the ground, so there would be no trace. He told them they had known another wizard long ago who could do that. But they didn't think it could be him. They had heard he had died in the wars. Galtenga chimed in at this point and told them they had found only his dragon, back broken, impaled on a sharpened tree trunk. He died shortly after. A blood trail had led away and finally disappeared downstream in the river. Even though they had searched for him, they had never again seen Garvin, the old man. They argued about telling this latest development to those back in Ashwind. Still, Conall didn't want to tell the Guardian, didn't want to open the old wound until they were sure. They decided for now not to alert the Guardian and they would resume their search. Once they flew across the river, they would continue on foot looking for anything that showed what had happened to Banprionsa, hoping to keep finding the tracks of the sandals.

They had been searching all day with no success when Ainmire looked behind him and saw a dust cloud in the distance. He brought it to the attention of Banríoncruba and with his eyesight of an eagle, he could tell them there was a rider on a speckled horse coming this way. They hoped the rider could divulge more information about the area and give them some idea of where someone might live in the mountains.

"I think we should stop and wait for whoever is riding this way," said Tristan.

"We need water and food. So, I agree. Let's see if we can learn anything," said Ainmire.

As Tegan crossed the river, this time with no problems, she realized that the search party was in front of her. She thought about galloping right by them, but quickly discarded that decision; it might make them suspicious. As she came near them, she slowed her horse to a walk and finally stopped near Tristan. She dismounted and, without showing surprise at the dragons, asked if they were the searchers from Ashwind. Tristan nodded, and she explained she had just come from there. Tegan told them with so much pride that she was now bonded to a dragon. Its feathers were the color of a ripe pumpkin. From the description, the two dragons knew it was Gearcleite.

They smiled at the young girl's excitement and didn't notice the mind shield she had thrown up. Her Grandfather had taught her well.

"Do you know of anyone who lives in the mountains?" said the Wizard.

"I've heard stories of an old man they say who wanders the hills. Some even say he is a wizard. I'm not sure that I believe that."

Tegan kept eye contact the whole time she spoke. That way, they would not pick up on the lie she had told. She knew that her trip this afternoon would require a stop at her aunt's, warning her in case they came to her village.

"Where are you riding to?" asked Tristan.

"My aunt lives in a village about an hour's ride from here."

She told them of her aunt's village. That the center revolved around a well that always had the clearest blue water running through it. Every family grew a specific crop. They grew wheat, while the neighbors to one side grew corn and, on the other, tomatoes that sometimes grew larger than melons. The village had a common chicken coop that all could take eggs from. Two cows provided milk for all. Every weekend, the hunting parties would go out and shoot deer, rabbits and wild boar, whichever they could find to feed the village for that week. Women and children would wander the lowlands in search of berries and spices that grew wild. Some they would use to cook and eat. They used others for healing, though she was still learning the difference. She shared her worries that her family might not fare as well if she was gone too much.

"I need to get going. I told the Guardian I would let him know if my aunt would let me join the school."

"I am Ainmire and I'm a teacher at the school. If it would help, I could speak to your aunt."

"Thank you, but I'm not sure it would. My uncle is missing and she might be worried that without him and me, there won't be enough help to get food."

"I'm sure the Guardian can help if he needs to. He's done that for several others. Once we find the missing girls, I will speak to him."

"Thank you Ainmire. I'm sure my aunt would appreciate it."

"May you have the speed of the gray wolf and may mother earth keep you safe on your journey," said Ainmire.

"I'll see you when we return and introduce you to my friends. The girls will definitely be happy to have another friend to add to their number," said Tristan.

After Tegan left, the Wizard looked at the others. He spoke and then stopped himself.

"Ainmire, did she seem nervous?" asked Tristan.

"Wizard, what did you see?"

"It could just be we're strangers. It felt like she was hiding something."

"Yes, I agree. Was it only how poor they are? Something more about the missing uncle? Or does she know more about the girls? I couldn't get a good read," said Ainmire.

"We won't figure it out right now. I think we should keep going," said Tristan.

The searchers were tired and hungry. They had not gotten far that day. Only a few miles but, as they occasionally saw what looked like a chain being dragged along the ground, they were confident they were going in the right direction. Here, they found an imprint that must be Banprionsa's. They halted for the night. Other than the girl, they had seen nobody on the road. Her village must be an outpost that was set up during the war, or so Galtenga told them, and Conall nodded his agreement.

Tristan told the others he needed time for himself and headed into the hills to walk and try to decide what to do. He wanted to take his sister home, to keep her safe, to watch her grow up. He didn't want her to be trapped by a madman and held captive. She was just a little girl. What evil would take a child? His head down, he walked. Tristan didn't see the buds just poking through the soil as if they were forcing themselves up to reach the sun's rays. He didn't see the fledgling eagles soar to a new branch, showing off to his brothers what they had not yet dared to try. Tristan didn't see the fawn eating the grass just off to the meadow on the right, while its mother stood guard just feet away. He didn't see the old man walking the hills near him until he was no longer in hailing range.

When Tristan finally focused on what was around him, he realized the sun was just going to drop behind the highest peak. The wind had turned cool, and he knew he should get back to the others. As he turned to go, his eyes caught a figure in the distance, cloaked, so it was challenging to say man or woman, though something about it said man to him. He gave a hello hoping to attract attention, but the trees absorbed it and he couldn't even hear an echo. With that, he turned, retraced his steps and rejoined the others.

As Tristan entered the camp, he smelled rabbit that was being turned on a spit. He had forgotten the amazing scent of rabbit cooking over an open fire. He saw Conall had vegetables roasting and that the dragons, judging by the scattered fur and feathers, had found and eaten their food.

"Have a good walk? See anybody?" said Conall.

"I saw a figure, but they were too far away to tell if they were male or female. I tried to hail him, but I guess he couldn't hear."

At that, the dragons took off and headed the way Tristan had come. With their superior eyesight, they might find whomever Tristan had seen. They were only gone a short while before they returned.

Ay spotted a trail, but thare were no people, said Oracruba. *We will try again in the morning.*

Conall, Ainmire and Tristan sat down and ate their dinner. They stored the leftovers for the morning. The stars came out when Tristan finally asked.

Why were you exiled?

I don't enjoy talking about it, Conall said.

Tell them the story, our version, said Galtenga.

I'm not sure they will understand.

If ye d'noo try, ye won't ever ken.

Conall turned and stared at Tristan and then Ainmire for a moment. Ainmire refused to break eye contact and nodded for Conall to start.

There were six of us and we had a couple of days off from training. Which we spent in the forest. On our return, we spotted those we called the Others. Garvin and I wanted to talk to them, but the Guardian forced us all to go back to Castle Farraige. He went to the council of the elders and shared what we had seen. Once he had left us for the council, Garvin and I headed back out with Luchcruba and Galtenga to see if we could talk to the Others.

The four walked to the outer ring of the castle, then soared into the air. They headed toward the next village before circling out toward the sea where they had spotted the group marching. They rode high among the clouds and were surprised by the number of creatures they saw on the road. There were men as tall as small trees; there were creatures that looked like the etchings they had seen of trolls and what might be dragons that swam in the sea instead of flying or burrowing.

We should head back, and tell them what we have seen, said Luchcruba.

Let's try to speak to them. See if they know the common tongue, said Garvin. *Maybe they've come for trade.*

I agree with Garvin, said Conall.

Conall, ye always agree with him. It usually means trouble, said Galtenga.

True, but let's do it, anyway.

The four glided down toward the convoy. As they neared it, they looked for who seemed in charge. One of the throng constantly waved his arms about and shouted so loudly the clouds could hear. They winged their way toward that person. As they got closer, they found a porcupine of weapons trained on them. They quickly flapped to a safer height, flew ahead and waited for the Others on the hard-packed road, just before it went around the next bend. There, a group of five of the strangers left the main body and approached them on foot. They told us that a plague had blighted their lands and they were looking for a new place where they could live in peace. The four told them they would fly ahead and inform the King at Castle Farraige.

They winged their way directly back to the Castle and found the Guardian waiting for them. His face turned a dark red.

How can you be so irresponsible to go without permission? asked the Guardian.

Do you want to know what they told us, or just yell at us? asked Garvin.

Go ahead.

They say their lands are no longer fit to live in and they are looking for a new place to live in peace.

Garvin, do you really believe this? You can be so naïve, said the Guardian.

Just because I found out, and you didn't, doesn't make it wrong, said Garvin.

No, but you believe anything anyone tells you. I thought you would have known better, Conall.

Then we had a huge fight. The four of us went and joined the Others. We thought to help them find a place to live. If we stayed with them, maybe they would appreciate us. By the time we realized the Guardian was right, the war had started and we were stuck. Eventually I change sides, but it was too late.

So, they have ostracized you all these years, said Tristan.

Aye, it was the law of both our cultures. They could hae killed us, but we served on their side in the end. So, we lived, said Fadcruba.

I'm tired. It's time we sleep so we can get an early start tomorrow, said Conall.

15

Chapter 15—The Questions

After his walk in the woods, the old man reentered the cave, shaking his head. He worried about his granddaughter; Tegan should have been back several hours ago. He hoped they had not captured her. That the Guardian had not figured out who she belonged to. But no, he would not. To his brother, he was dead and had been since the day he had gone to the other side to fight. He had left the two captives stewing long enough. They should have been fully awake at this point.

The girls had discussed it and decided that Siona would ask the questions. She could make her eyes water, like she had tears, just by pinching herself. It worked with her brothers; maybe it would work with the old man. As the old man walked into where the girls were, Siona spoke up, tears brimming from her eyes.

"Who are you? Why have you brought us here? I have to go to the bathroom."

"Huh," he made an insignificant gesture, like flicking away dust. Siona's chains cha-ching'd into a pile at her feet. He pointed her to a curtained area.

Siona walked in and realized that there was a girl who lived here. There were brushes and a pretty mirror near the granite wash basin. She was less frightened knowing that there would be a girl here at some point.

Unless she had been a captive too.

Siona's head flicked back and forth, quick as a bird's, as she scanned for signs of the girl's recent presence. There was nothing to say if it was yesterday or last winter. Now she really needed the toilet.

When she stepped back through the curtain, she didn't immediately return to Banprionsa. The old man watched as Siona wandered around, looking at the cooking knives. He knew she was wondering if she could get one and hide it without him seeing her. She touched the table and ran her hand over the cotton cloth that had covered the bread. Her mouth watered and her stomach grumbled. Just as she reached for a small knife, he tired of waiting for her.

"Girl, what are you doing? Get back to your place on the wall."

"My name is *Siona*. What's yours?"

"Garvin."

"Why are we here?"

Garvin looked at her, trying to decide how much to tell this child. She was here because he sought vengeance. He wanted to take from them what they had taken from him long ago.

"Revenge."

With that, the old man reattached her bonds, then he turned and left. He should have known better than to give them his name. What was he thinking? He needed to remember that they were not Tegan. They belonged to the people he had sworn to hate. Those that had kept him an outcast. They had given him up for dead and now he was ready to make them pay. He could not let those girls know they had broken through his defenses so easily.

The old man headed into the forest. He would check on the wolf he had guarding the woods. Make sure he was still under his thrall. He would pick up some vegetables to keep on hand. Dragons, he knew from experience, weren't partial to them, but if hungry enough, they would eat them.

Siona and Banprionsa looked at each other as the old man left the room.

What do you think he meant by revenge? Siona said.

Must be agin the two-footed races. Agin somebody from the village. Thay hinna seen dragons for a long time.

Yeah, but against who?

The girls talked, going over and over the same ideas. Not truly understanding what the old man had meant. Then they veered off into how he could use them for what he wanted. What would he do to them? They just couldn't figure it out. After a while, they fell silent. Each went into her own thoughts, Siona on how to get information and Banprionsa on how to escape. She understood more than Siona about what could happen. She had learned from listening to stories of war. Banprionsa thought this might be like a minor war and they would sacrifice captives: them. She kept thinking about escaping. What they should do to survive.

Banprionsa leaned toward Siona and whispered her scheme for escape. She reminded her of what they had observed that morning. The old man went out and left them alone for at least an hour. If Siona left shortly after that, then she could get a head start. Siona told Banprionsa she would not depart without her, that nothing could make her do so.

Besides, I don't know where we are and I won't be able to bring back help. The old man might hurt you if I escape. If anyone should go, it should be you.

Siona, it will take a lot mare for him to hurt me than ye. Which is why ye need to go. Just pick a direction and get to the naurer village.

Right, and if I tell them a crazy man kidnapped my dragon and me, they would think I was crazy.

Ye could just ask them to contact the Guardian. It seems like everybody ken him.

Well, it doesn't matter, because I'm not going.

At that Siona, turned her head and sniffled. Banprionsa didn't give up. She explained to Siona how people might not have seen a dragon yet and she wouldn't be able to communicate with them. They might try to kill her because she would look strange. If Siona showed up at a village, they would help her. It wouldn't matter what story she told.

Siona just kept shaking her head no and would discuss nothing with Banprionsa. This was the first time the girls had disagreed. Each entrenched in their own idea, the cave became quiet as a tomb. There was one thing that Banprionsa said that had Siona worried. Nobody knew where they were. Siona kept her back to Banprionsa, even when the old man returned.

"Now I think this should do it. I'm going to have to try it on the dragon to see how much damage it will do."

The old man realized he had been muttering to himself. He looked over and noticed that the dragon appeared to be sleeping, although the child watched his every move. Her face didn't seem to have changed, but he wondered if she had heard him.

Putting his back to the girl, he whispered, "Not now. I'll give it to the dragon on her meat with dinner. Then I will know what might happen. Not enough to kill her... just yet."

The old man could not stand how silent the cave had been since his return. He missed the constant chatter of his granddaughter. Tegan looked just like the daughter who highway men had murdered. She had been the one child to understand him. He loved his other children, but they did not comprehend his need to pay back the hurt he had felt for the loss he suffered. It was their fault that he couldn't go back to his kind, that he must practice in secret.

He glanced over at the two he held, wondering at their silence. Their constant chatter had been so much like his Tegan's that it kept him from missing her. He questioned the cessation of their incessant blather and the glares that were passing between them. He felt their anger, which was blocking their thoughts from him. But he was not used to the silence, and wanted their babble much like a mother bird wanted the song of her chicks, so she knew where they were.

Talk, said the old man.

What? Came to his mind and ears at the same time.

I want you to talk.

"About what?" said Siona.

"I don't care. Tell me about your families."

He asked this not so much because he cared, but so the quiet would not overwhelm him.

Siona and Banprionsa were still mad at each other, but quickly decided that Siona would tell the tale. She started by telling him about her parents dying...

The old man shook his head and looked at the girl as her story wound down.

"... and that's how I came to live at the castle and with my new mum and dad."

Shaking his head, the old man wondered why he had asked; now the girl was a person and not an object to be used. He marveled at the sweetness and steel he had seen in her. She was like his Tegan; not bent from the loss that she had suffered. He realized this was going to make it harder to use her as a tool of revenge, but he wasn't ready to give it up.

Siona looked at him and told him it was Banprionsa's turn to tell her family story. She warned him it might make him sad. It had made her sad the first time she had heard it. Banprionsa glanced at her friend and sent thanks to her. It was the first time in hours the girls had connected.

Knowing it was his fault and that he had started their chatter, he nodded at the two girls and told the dragon to tell her tale and get it over with. Banprionsa began by saying what he never thought would be the first words out of her mouth. "My mither died giein birth to me..."

The girl, Siona, had been right. This story was sad.

...and though Ay hae ken for a while that my biological Grandfaither, Galtenga, is alive, Ay hae n'er met him. Ay really would like to someday, but Ay d'noo want to hurt Dubhbragh, who raised me and is really my faither.

The old man sat there, stunned. Galtenga alive? How could that be? He was the brother of his own long missed dragon. They had fought together in the war. The stories, if this girl was right, had been wrong. Did that mean the wizard lived too? Could he recruit them to his side? He needed to decide how to proceed. He knew if he harmed Galtenga's grandchild, there was no way the dragon and the wizard would join him. Tegan had said their fathers were coming. Did that mean Dubhbragh was on his way? He had to think. He got up without a word and left the cave.

The Old Man fretted over where that granddaughter of his had gotten to. He would walk his hills and think. He would not react in haste, as he had in the past. The tools of vengeance were in his hands, but they had become more than that through their stories. He should have never listened to them talk. It had just made things harder. He would not give up on his retaliation just because they had become real to him. He had waited too long for this chance.

Even his granddaughter didn't know his actual age and just how long he had waited for this, how long he had been alone until he had married his Farah. He should never have allowed himself to fall for that girl, marry and have children. That was the start of his downfall. That was when his heart had thawed. Ah, but if he hadn't, he wouldn't have Tegan now, and that thought was too much to bear.

Banprionsa watched the old man leave. He had been visibly upset by her tale. She looked at Siona, and the two immediately put aside their earlier disagreement.

Ay think he ken something about me.

Yeah, I think he does too.

Ay need ye to help me suss it out.

I want to, but you're right, we need to escape.

Ay d'noo think we're actually in danger just yet. We can wait for one more day. Then speik about it again. First, Ay need to ken what he ken.

No, while you slept, he talked about that horrid smelling stuff. It's to hurt dragons. He plans on giving you some at dinner. He said something about it not being enough to kill you. We can't wait. I can't let him hurt you.

The girls spent the next several hours trying to figure out the best way to escape. They came up with one ridiculous idea after the other. Their ideas bounced around like a rock tumbling down a hill until they finally ran out and just started going over the same ones again. Banprionsa stopped talking abruptly.

Hush, I think he is comin.

Not more than a minute later did the old man walk in. He looked tired and sad. The girls almost felt sorry for him. Before either of them said anything, Siona's stomach growled. Without even a glance at them, he commented they must be hungry and prepared food for them. Rabbit, again. But at least it tasted good. They hadn't been there long enough to be tired of it yet. He sliced vegetables. Siona offered her help. She told him that Emmair, her new mother, was teaching her to cook, and she knew how to chop, so if he wanted, she could help.

"Don't need help," said the old man.

"Do you have a daughter?"

"Yes."

"What's she like?"

"Why do you want to know?"

"Well, we told you all about our families, so you should tell us about yours."

"Nothing to tell."

"Are they all dead?"

"No, not all. Now stop asking these questions. Can't you see I'm busy?"

"But, I just..."

"No more questions," said the old man. As he chopped through a carrot and hit the cutting board with so much force, it made a thud.

He finished his cutting and started preparing the rabbit. With a little help from magic, he had it simmering and cooked in just under an hour.

After giving Siona a steaming bowl, he returned to the fireplace with a larger bowl. He ladled stew into it, then stepped to his left between the captives and the pot holding the putrid potion. The Old Man bent forward, paused for a moment, then straightened. He returned to the girls gingerly carrying the bowl, which he sat on the floor in front of the dragon. Then he rushed toward the cave entrance.

"Where are you going?" said Siona.

"To look for my granddaughter. She's late."

Why did I answer the girl? She's not Tegan. I can't keep giving them information. It's as if my words are like the wind that whipped through the trees, uncontrolled.

Once as he was gone, Siona grabbed the bowl he had given Banprionsa and moved it out of her way. The dragon went back to work on getting the chain loose from the wall. She used the point of her claw to dig around the rock. The wall wasn't as strong there because of the spike he had hastily hammered into the existing fissure. It didn't take as long as the girls had expected, and Siona could pull the barb out.

Let me get you fresh food.

Siona, dump what he gave me back into the pot he got it from. That way, we don't have to figure out what to do with it.

Good idea. How are we going to cover up the hole?

Ay d'noo hae the words to explain whit Ay'm gaun to do once ye hae the spike back in place.

Siona crammed the chain back in its place. Banprionsa scooped up a hand full of dust from her excavation. Holding it in her scaled palm, she breathed a whisper of flame onto the egg size mound. The dust melted and congealed just enough to provide a mortar, to secure the chain back in the wall. The two moved to cover the expanded hole and the loosened pebbles that now sprinkled the cave floor.

Now that Siona was free, they decided she would make her escape the next morning. It wouldn't be good for her to wander around a place she didn't know at night. Banprionsa could hear the footsteps of the old man as he exited the cave. As they crossed the veil of water, the dragon no longer could trace his steps. She hoped this would help Siona know when to go.

16

Chapter 16 - The Showdown

Tegan arrived at her aunt's and flung herself out of the saddle. Her younger brother and sister barreled down on her from the front porch. She grabbed them to her and hugged them. She could hardly believe how much they had grown. They kept repeating over and over how much they missed her.

She played tag, read them a story and helped her aunt cook the evening meal. Tegan asked after her uncle, who had gone to trade furs in a village further east. She was told there had been no word of him, but he might have stopped to visit with his sister. They had talked about that before he left. Kyna had, however, heard rumors of a band of brigands raiding in the area and worried about her husband.

Her aunt once again told her she should stay with them and not live with her grandfather in a cave. Her aunt stated she didn't understand how the old man could have moved there, let alone dragged Tegan with him. She patiently told her aunt how much she enjoyed it. But, as her aunt launched into yet another tirade, she was quick to add, "I was at the castle earlier today and they have asked me to join the school."

Her aunt squealed with excitement. She had heard of the school and thought it would be the best thing for Tegan. As she took a breath, she asked Tegan what her grandfather had said.

"I have not told him yet."

"I see. If he says 'no' you come and tell me. If you want to go, I'll see that you do."

Nodding, she said goodbye to her brother and sister. Giving everyone a last hug, she headed back to the mountains, to her grandfather. As she rode beneath the half-moon, she watched the stars in the sky. She looked for the mother's cup and the belt of father's moon. She noticed how the shadows made the cloudless night look frightening. In the rock, she saw shapes of bears, coyotes. Her horse reared when a snake crossed its path, heading for the warmth of the lower caves. The trail was slick as she headed upward toward the waterfall and home. Just beyond the veil of the falls, she could make out a shape she knew so well. Tegan urged her mare forward and quickly dismounted when she was just a few feet away. After a quick hug, she jumped right in.

"Grandfather, I have something to tell you."

Tegan patted her horse's flank and led her inside. Before she got two steps, her grandfather stopped her.

"Where have you been, Tegan?"

"I went to see the little ones. It might be some time before I can see them again."

"Why? You can go anytime."

"I know, but things are different now."

"How?"

"Well, you know the dragons are back?"

"Yes, and I told you to stay far away from them?" said the old man, looking at her, as if he couldn't believe what he knew must be forthcoming.

"I know you told me to stay away, but I just couldn't. I felt drawn to this one dragon, and it was like I couldn't help myself. When I touched the dragon, it glowed gold. I have bonded with it."

"No, you will stay away from the castle. You can't ever go back there again."

"Grandfather, we need to talk about this."

“No, we don’t. You will do as you are told.”

“I am not a child that you can just order around.”

“Yes, you are. Now get your horse and let’s go inside. I don’t want to hear any more of this.”

“I am going back to the castle and unless you are going to put a spell on me, there is nothing you can do to stop me.”

“Go inside. We’ll get dinner and then maybe I can talk some sense into you.”

Without waiting for an answer, the old man turned his back on her and stomped back into the cave. But before he got too far, he waved his hand at his granddaughter and said some words that changed her appearance. She finished taking care of the horse and walked into the cave, where for the first time she came in contact with Siona and Banprionsa. It surprised her when she saw the chains holding them captive.

“Is that your granddaughter?” said Siona.

“Yes.”

“She seems older than I expected.”

“He’s put a spell on me so you can’t see who I am or hear my proper voice.”

“You don't need to tell them anything. Help finish dinner.”

“What are your names?”

“I’m Siona and this is Banprionsa.”

“Alright, I’ll help you finish.”

Tegan looked at her grandfather and could tell by the set of his shoulders that he was unhappy. She quickly finished slicing the bread. She gave food first to the captives and then dished up for herself and her grandfather.

“I wish to eat under the stars. Will you join me, Grandfather?”

“I will not.”

“Please.”

The two headed out to the mouth of the cave and went to their usual spots; they had sat there so many times that the rocks had worn down with the imprint of their backsides. They ate in silence and Tegan looked at the stars. She liked it when the sky was clear and it seemed as if the stars were chasing each other across the sky. She was quiet for so long that her grandfather took a peek to see if she had fallen asleep. He knew he needed to talk to her about this dragon business. He suspected he had already lost her to the castle.

"Grandfather, you have not lost me."

"I didn't say I had."

"I know you were thinking it. I know what has to be done. If I'm there, I'm going to help you more."

"How?"

"I won't have to go in disguise. I can be myself and people will just talk in front of me."

"They won't let you leave whenever you want."

"I've taken care of that. I can go early Monday mornings and come home on Fridays."

"They will never let you."

"I told the Guardian I couldn't come to the school because I had to help my family."

"You spoke to the Guardian? Did he recognize you?"

"Why would he recognize me? He is the enemy. Though he seemed very nice."

"Girl, you must not trust him. He will turn on you in a minute. He is why you can't go back, ever."

"I am going back, so please let's not fight."

"Tegan, you don't understand how treacherous he is."

"How would you know when you've never been to the village?"

"He's my brother and the reason I have had to live in hiding."

"Your brother? How can that be? What did he do to you?"

"You remember the stories of the great war?"

"Yes."

"I was on the opposite side of the war. The people who were supposed to be my friends never listened to anything I said. Especially my brother. There was a great air battle on dragons and the Guardian and I ended up fighting each other. Magic, arrows, curses were all thrown at each other. He hit my Luchcruba, who went down. She spiraled into a tree that was sharpened like a spike. It pierced her armor and went through her heart. She died within minutes. I was flung far enough away that I was uninjured and unseen. My brother never even looked."

"I'm sorry Grandfather, I know this is difficult for you."

"Tegan, don't say anymore, sleep on it and decide in the morning. Know your decision will change your whole life."

Tegan slept restlessly that night and only went into a deep slumber as the sun woke the new day. She didn't hear the captives move about.

Banprionsa was the first to stir in the morning. She nudged at Siona's mind. *Wake-up Siona.*

Siona wiped her eyes and turned to look at her friend. *Just because dragons don't need as much sleep..*

Will ye shut up? Look over at the girl.

What about her?

The tips of her hair hae changed.

You're right, the tips look white-blond, not red like last night. Where have I seen that color before?

Stay still. Maybe she willnae wauk up right awa. We might see it cheenge completely.

But just as she finished that thought, the old man woke. The girls closed their eyes before he realized they were awake.

"Girl, it's time to get up."

"Thanks, Grandfather."

"What have you decided?"

"I know you won't be happy, but I've decided I have to go back. I will come and see you as often as I can. That I promise," said Tegan as she clenched her hand hoping he wouldn't see it tremble.

"No! You are not welcome here any longer," as her grandfather's hand slammed down onto the counter.

"What are you saying?"

"You are dead to me. No longer my granddaughter."

"Grandfather, you can't mean that," said Tegan as tears fell from her eyes like rain.

"I mean it, you've made your decision and I've made mine. Now go," said her Grandfather his voice shaking as he turned her back too him.

The two hadn't realized that the captives were awake and had heard all that had transpired. They could hardly believe what they had just heard. Siona decided she had better say something before he caught them. She opened her eyes and gave an enormous yawn, stretching out as far as she could.

"Are you leaving so soon?" Siona said. Both the old man and the girl jumped. They thought the two were asleep. "Where are you going?"

"Home. I promised my aunt I would help with the little ones today."

The old man looked surprised for one second and then nodded.

"She can be impatient that one, so you had better hurry."

"My new mum can be that way too."

"New mum?" said Tegan.

"My parents died when I was very young. Emmair and Cadryn adopted my brothers and I."

"You need to get going, girl."

"Yes, Grandfather. Will you walk me out?"

"No, I'm busy."

Tegan gave him a fierce hug that he didn't return. She knew she had to go, although it saddened her he could be this angry. She would come back when she had information, and Tegan was sure he would forgive her.

Moments after Tegan's departure, the old man shouldered his sack and left the cave. Siona looked at Banprionsa and silently shared the thought that they should try now.

Okay, Siona, he is out of the cave. Ye should ga now.

Talk to me all the way out, will you?

Aye, but ga now.

Siona pulled the nail out of the wall and headed toward the cave entrance. She peered carefully around each corner, even though she believed he was not here. She had rounded the third corner when Banprionsa screamed into her mind.

Run back. He's inside the cave.

Without hesitation, Siona spun and raced back to Banprionsa. They didn't have time to put the nail back into the wall, but they sat in such a way that it didn't show. When the old man walked in, he heard them grumbling about being hungry.

"I forgot my bow. I'm going out again, now."

"Can we have breakfast?"

He didn't say a word, but threw them a loaf of bread and some cheese. With that, he turned, grabbed the small bow and arrows, then headed back out.

Siona waited several minutes longer than before. She didn't want to risk discovery if she could help it. At Banprionsa's urging, she took some of the bread and cheese, wrapped it in a cloth and once again started for the cave's entrance. This time she had made it. Siona could feel the spray of the water, and she was just heading over to the path around the water when she saw the old man. She ducked back behind the water and scrambled toward the cave entrance. She wasn't certain what would happen if he caught her, but it wouldn't be good. Just before she reached the innermost cavern, she felt him grab her arm. He flung her around and seized her throat. His eyes bored, silent fury into hers. He shook her like she was a jackrabbit whose neck he was going to break.

He roughly spun her back around and grabbed her by the nape. He marched her across the floor and secured her once again. His face was the color of a red magic lily, veins stood out and pulsed. He reached out and pulled down a book with pages so old the girls had never seen the paper they made it from. He studied each spell carefully, searching for some specific incantation. When he flipped the pages, it sounded like old leaves being trod on. He found a clean pot and gathered ingredients from shelves and cabinets around the chamber. These he ground together in a stone mortar. Then he threw them in the boiling water, all the time mumbling words under his breath. When he had completed the task, he poured the liquid into a cup.

"Drink it." The old man growled, shoving the goblet toward Siona.

When she refused, he whispered some words, her eyes rolling up in her head. Without conscious thought, she took the glass and drank the contents. Siona gagged and her stomach roiled. She looked at her friend for help. Then green fire flowed like flaming honey from Banprionsa's mouth. Siona shrieked as the mucus colored magma poured into her throat. Her insides were melting, like the ice in the pond, when the sun was at its zenith. Her lungs seared as the river of fire poured into them. The agony was so profound that she wished that each breath was her last. She could hear the old man cackling.

"You'll think again before you try to get away."

Siona's fingers formed claws as she tried to tear the burning skin away like it was a boiling tar. She flapped her arms, kicked her feet. She soiled herself and as it expelled from her, it felt as if all of her insides had become molten.

Banprionsa watched as Siona writhed on the cave floor. As their link was so strong, she could feel what her friend was going through. She knew that there was no fire. That it was only an illusion, but she feared that madness might take her before it wore off. Her heart tore out of her as Siona screamed.

Banprionsa, why are you doing this to me?

Siona, listen to me. Come on, Siona. Ay am noo doing this. Tis magic. The drink, do ye remember the drink?

Yes, he said it would help to keep you from burning me.

Siona, fight it. Say to yourself it's not real. Say it, Siona!

This is not real. Banprionsa is not trying to kill me.

Think, Siona, about a cool, clear river. That one near the castle ye told me tasted like pine nuts. Go to the stream in yer mind. Can ye do that?

I can see the water, but it's on fire.

No Siona, tis yer brothers playing tricks. The water is still cool. Can ye drink from the water?

Too scared.

Drink NOW SIONA, DRINK now!

Siona bent her head as if to put it under water. She made a sucking sound, like she was taking in the water.

Are ye cooling off now, Siona?

Yes.

17

Chapter 17 - FOP at Work

As the sun had just crested the hill behind Dragon Alley, a small group stood in the castle's shadow where none could see their faces. Their backs were against the castle wall and they stood facing out, watching the two-footed interact with those dragons that were out. They continually looked around, like scared mice searching for a cat.

"Do you think the girl will come back?" said Nessa.

"She touched a dragon, and it glowed. She'll be back," Carin said.

"Yes, but will she join us or them?"

"You need to make friends with her. Learn what you can before we approach her."

"I'm not good at making friends. The girls rarely like me."

"Nessa, stop making excuses. You're going to have to figure it out. Talk about dragons. It seems like that's all anyone wants to do, anyway. She is new here and will need a friend."

The girl nodded.

"What are we going to do now?" asked The Mountain. "Should I go take care of the equipment?"

"No, I think I had better do that. The dragons are used to seeing me around, but they aren't used to seeing you," said Carin. "Hopefully, when the next group arrives, you will find your dragon."

"Do you think so?"

"We have to hope. You're of pure blood and should have been one of the first. What you need to do is tell those that don't have dragons all the horror stories you have heard. Maybe it will keep the half-breeds and the non-humans away from them."

"They should never let them touch them. The sub-humans have kept some of us from getting dragons. That should never have happened," said Nessa.

"Well, it did," Carin said. "I'm off to the caves. You both get busy."

The Mountain and Nessa watched as Carin sauntered over toward the cave. Nessa noticed how her cousin effortlessly spoke to all he encountered. Carin hid his disdain for the lesser beings easily. Everyone thought he was their friend. He had explained that this way he would know what was going on. That way, he could know who to target and who could be used to their advantage.

The Mountain headed over to a group of younger children gathered together under a yew tree. As he arrived, he overheard one dwarf boy say he heard that more dragons would come the next day. Several of the group mentioned they wanted to be one of the first to touch them. They hoped they would bond with one of them. This gave the Mountain his opening.

"Why would you want to bond with them?" said the Mountain.

"We want to fly."

"And what happens when you are hundreds of feet up in the air and slip out of the saddle? You end up looking like a large crushed cockroach. Your guts spilled everywhere and there's a good chance nobody will know who you are."

"That doesn't happen."

"Really, didn't you see one of those boys who get to fly have his saddle slip around? If he hadn't been close to the ground, he would have been smashed like a cockroach," said the Mountain.

"He should have checked his equipment better. Even he said that."

"Yes, even a slight mistake on one of these creatures can kill you," said the Mountain. "Did you see the girl with her arm burned yesterday?"

The group shook their heads no.

"Well, it looked like cooked meat. I guess she pissed off her dragon, and the animal set her on fire. They get mean when they don't get their way. Not sure why anyone would want to ride one."

With that, the Mountain walked away. For once, he realized if he said more, it might be too much.

Though Carin couldn't see what the Mountain had said from where he stood near the entrance to the dragon armory, he could see the children nervously milling about. He nodded to himself, hoping that what the Mountain said had scared some of them off. Carin turned away and took the few steps toward the armory entrance. He glanced around to make sure that nobody was watching and headed inside.

A couple of days before, he had tried to sabotage Pogee's saddle. Unfortunately, it had come loose too soon, and the boy had tumbled harmlessly to the ground. You wouldn't have thought so the way Emmair, his mother, had shrieked like a barn owl. Carin had a different target today. He knew that the elf, Aine, would ride soon. Her uncle, Ainmire, was teaching the riders, so he was certain Aine would be one of the first to ride. He looked around, knowing elves favored the color green. He spotted a saddle that was the green of a spring meadow. An engraved and painted tree of life spiraled up from the stirrups to the horn. It was one solid piece. There were others, but what made him sure that this was the right one was the small crown with real rubies that adorned the opposite side. Only elves would put precious stones as decorations on a saddle. Carin wondered if he could find fake stones and replace them with the real ones. Then he shook his head. That wasn't what he was here for. He took out a knife and worked on the stitching.

18

Chapter 18 - The Ancient

Dubhbragh was pacing the field. He needed to do something. Oh, he understood that training was essential and if it had been a different time, he would have enjoyed it a great deal. Right now, his mind was on Banprionsa. He worried he hadn't paid enough attention to young Pogee. He could have been hurt when the strap came apart. Funny that it had. Everything seemed so well maintained.

Ay need to ga to the woods, said Dubhbragh.

I know it's hard to focus, however, this is important, said the Guardian.

Do ye think Ay d'noo understand the importance? Banprionsa is important too and Ay'm gaun to ga talk to the Elder Oak.

Why?

She might talk to the other ancient trees and maybe thay can tell hus where the monster is that took the wee anes.

Interesting idea. I wonder if the Night Marchers might help too, said the Guardian.

The Night Marchers always want sommit in return. The price coud be very high, said Dubhbragh.

Others can finish this training session. I'll speak to Brydon and we'll go.

The Guardian walked over to Brydon and explained what they were going to do.

"Guardian, instead of you and the dragon going, I think you should let me, Westerly and Aine go."

"Why?"

"The Elder Oak really likes Westerly and will probably help if he asks. After all, he is her Prince of Ceol."

"What about the Night Marchers?" asked the Guardian.

"Well, the old soldier owes me a favor or two for moving some of his people across. This seems like a good use of that favor. Besides, Siona is my sister, and I need to help."

The children entered the Winds forest, the path they walked to the elven altar was now easy to trod. It took them only the time to sing three songs. The Ancient knew of their approach, since the children always sang as they walked through the woods. Today's songs, though, weren't the usual cheery tunes the Prince of Ceol played. These had a bit of sadness and even fear in them. She wondered if what she had heard was true. Someone had taken a child.

The children stopped at the entrance to the altar stone. They waited to be acknowledged. Whenever they came, they could feel the spirit of the ancient tree that stood to the right of the altar stone. Its old trunk withered and scarred with age, like the lava fields with their folds, wrinkled and cracked. The tree was the embodiment of the spirit of this forest. Though old, she had more knowledge than all of them. The power she contained outstripped that of any man.

"Prince of Ceol, I see you have brought your friends with you this time. It is good to see you again, Soul Talkers."

"May we enter?" said Westerly.

"You may. I have heard the dragons are back. Is it true?"

"Yes, and we're very excited. All of us have bonded with a dragon. It's cool. Everything is going well."

"Not the entire truth, but we will go with that for the moment. Now, why have you come here?"

"Someone has taken my sister and her dragon. There are people searching; however, they have had no luck locating the children," said Brydon.

At that, Aine sent a picture of them. She saw that Banprionsa and Siona had been speaking through the winds since they had been born. That the two had only met in physical form a couple of days ago. But they were bonded more closely than many who had trained together for years.

"What can I do to help?"

"There are two things we might ask of you," said Westerly. "First, can you reach out to the Night Marcher's Old Soldier and get him to come here? He might help us."

"There will be a cost. He rarely does anything for free, but he owes you a favor, as I recall," said the Ancient. "I will call him and see if he will come."

At that, there was an uneasy quiet. Though no breeze was felt, they heard the leaves rustling in the trees as it moved away from them. Then the rustling came back toward them and the Ancient nodded to its trunk.

"He will come and hear you out."

A translucent man carrying a very solid sword walked into the clearing. He smelled slightly of rotting flesh and he came with anger shooting out of his eyes. It was easy to tell that he had no liking for being summoned, even by the Ancient.

"What do you want you, old piece of firewood?"

"It is not I who wish to speak to you, but those who are still among the living."

"You commanded me to come here because of them?"

"I don't believe I have ever 'commanded you.'"

Westerly's head kept swiveling back and forth like he was watching small children chase a ball that seemed to change hands or feet as smooth as water falling from gray clouds.

"So, what do you want from me?"

"A child, one human, one dragon, has been taken. We would like you to help find them," said Brydon.

"If I help you, what will you give me? How much is she worth to you?"

"Have you forgotten you owe us four future favors?"

"This is worth more than that. You will need to promise to move more of my people across."

With that, the breeze kicked up, and dust swirled. Leaves were thrown into the spirit. The ancient tree moved her trunk to loom over the old soldier. The limbs descended, but could not touch the specter.

"You are trading on the life of children. Children, all of them, are precious. Have you sunken so far as to have forgotten?"

"They are not children of my realm. So they don't matter to me. They are like the fall going to winter. They die and some come to me, others don't. If they die, I will help them."

"Go away, old man, your soul is rotting even worse than your flesh," said the Ancient

The children listened to the conversation and felt dismayed at the exchange. They knew spirits wouldn't help find the missing ones. The ancient tree moved back to its original position. The wind died down, and the dust settled. They stood there, not sure what to say. As the old solider turned and walked back into the forest, getting more translucent with each step.

"I see the old man may have finally lost some of his soul. We will need to figure out what is to be done about him.

"Thank you for trying to get him to help us," said Aine.

"You had another idea. Let me hear that. If I can help find the children, I will do so."

"We think you have a network of your own that you gather information from," said Westerly.

"Yes, but we aren't as concerned with precision as you might need us to be."

"We would ask if you hear of anything that seems off. You give us an idea of where we might need to look," said Westerly.

The Elder Oak was silent and all the forest around grew quiet. There was no rustle of leaves, not even the scurrying of small woodland creatures. The only sound was their own breathing.

"We will search and tell what we find. If a child requires help, the trees and plants will do what they can. The child, though, will have to be one that can hear the word of the winds. If not, it limits what we can do. Do you believe either child can hear the winds?" asked the Ancient.

"My sister is a dragon talker and she talked to the winds once," said Brydon.

"In times, past dragon talkers heard the winds. There may be hope," said the Ancient. "Brydon and Aine, you will come twice a day and I will give them news. Prince of Ceol, you have something else to do."

"What should I be doing?"

"Go to your room. Look at the map. Search there for the children. Have the others who have animal totems send them out to look. Ask for your room's essences. They will have other ideas. Talk to them."

"Thank you for your help and I will gather the guides and do as you suggest."

"Aine and I will be back in a few hours. We appreciate all your help in this," said Brydon.

With that, they bowed to the Ancient and watched as her bark closed up and she looked like just an ordinary tree.

19

Chapter 19 - The Rooms Speak

Westerly, Aine and Brydon went to the Guardian who was giving lessons to the Guides and their dragons. Westerly explained what the Ancient had suggested.

"Go take the guides and I will join one of the other groups. Aine, with Tristan gone, you go to the Lion Room and talk to the Princess. You, I understand, visit with her often. She likes you and I'm sure will at least listen to what you have to say," said the Guardian.

Dubhbragh sent a picture into the Guardian's mind of what he wanted him to say to the Guides.

"Dubhbragh, said to tell you that if there is a problem to let him know and he will speak to the dragon's essence."

Aine and all the Guides except Tristan headed toward the castle. As they walked away, Shaun came rushing up to them.

"Hey cousin, we're heading to the castle to talk to the essences," said Grady as he continued to the two-headed dog room.

"Hmm, I have an idea, but I want to get into Aunt Erin's cave. I think Grady should come with me."

"Why me? What idea?"

"The essences that I talk to. Some of them walk around here. They might help find Siona. Grady, I need you to help me. I might need extra power and I pissed one essence off. Remember?"

"Yep, he thought you were flirting with his girlfriend. Lame. But I need to talk to Donovan. You know the essence in my room. I could come when I'm done."

Shaun looked from Grady to Barra. Today, Barra was decked out as good as any female warrior could be. She had a bow over her shoulder and a short sword on her hip. Shaun saw she was shaking her head, and he wasn't sure which of them she was looking at.

"Grady, go with Shaun. The more people who are working on finding Siona and Banprionsa, the better. I'll tell Donovan."

"Barra, I think..."

"Go with Shaun. Donovan will be so proud of you. He'll know that you've put the needs of others over your own. This is a good thing."

Westerly had been walking behind and was watching the interchange between the three of them. He was so pleased that Barra had listened to the other girls and was trying to use persuasion instead of fists with her fellow warrior. They might even become good friends.

"Ok, come on, Shaun. Let's head back to the dragons and see if some of our new friends can give us a distraction."

With that, Westerly turned and watched Shaun and Grady head back to the training field.

"Well, Westerly, Grady's in his element for the moment. He has new friends to cause trouble with him," said Barra.

"Let's hope his dragon, Dubhcliete, helps. I think her name is 'will be calmer.'"

"We can only hope. But being female doesn't mean that you're calm."

With that, they entered the castle and headed to the library. The others were waiting by the fireplace for them to get there. Westerly quickly explained Grady's absence as they walked down the hallway. Westerly stopped at the Falcon room door, gave the secret word and they crowded into the closet and then his room. Once everyone sat, girls were on the bed and the boys lounging on chairs or the cushions on the floor. An extra cushion appeared as Westerly looked around for a place to sit.

"Thanks, Riley," said Westerly as he glanced at the wall.

"Alright Westerly, tell us what the Ancient asked us to do," said Dalton.

"She suggested we each talk to the essences in our rooms. Those with totems that are of animals might be able to send them out to speak to the animals they resemble."

"Our room doesn't have an animal," said Mirah.

"Mirah. I'm not sure about the tree, but you should talk to your essences too. They might have other ideas. Once everyone has talked to their room's essences, let's meet back here."

"Who's going to talk to the Lion Room's essence?" asked Mirah.

"Aine will talk to the Princess since Tristan is gone. It's what the Guardian suggested," said Westerly.

Before anyone else could speak, the door to Westerly's room opened, and a breeze came through the window, pushing the other occupants toward the door. Brydon was slow in getting up and the breeze that went toward him pushed him across the floor.

After the door closed behind the others, Westerly went to the wall with the map. Today it was showing Ashwind Castle and the surrounding area.

Riley, the Ancient said it could be possible for you to send the falcon out and have him talk to other birds. That they might have seen who took Siona and Banprionsa. Can you do that?

Yes, I can do that. Give me a moment.

Westerly perched on the bed and watched as the window open. He thought he saw the shadow of a falcon go out through it.

Riley, Ay think tis time we explain to Westerly about his magic, said Báncliete.

My magic? What magic?

Ye ken how on the map ye can see the different villages, said Báncliete.

Sure, the map gets bigger and I can see what's going on in specific places. But isn't that the magic of the map? asked Westerly.

Bird sight.

What?

Báncliete, would you like me to explain? asked Riley.

Go ahead. Ay'll fill in, if needed.

So, the map itself isn't magic? Westerly asked.

It is. Except the map can only show general areas. The falcon can take you close and show the details that you see.

But the others see it too. Do they all have bird sight?

No, they see it, Westerly, because you show it to them, said Riley.

Whit Riley means is that once ye see it, then it appears to anyone in the room. That's part of the map's magic, said Báncliete.

I still don't understand what that has to do with the falcon, said Westerly.

Báncliete, you'd better explain, said Riley.

Are ye sure?

Please, just one of you explain it to me.

There was silence, and Westerly walked over to the window. His room overlooked dragon alley. Usually, there was nothing to see unless someone was playing with a ball or sitting on the small mound having a picnic. Today was different. He now understood why the place was clear. To give the dragons room to take off and land. Below, he could see Pogee and Ryuu trying to climb up onto their dragons. Then he spotted Emmair and he could imagine what she was going to say to the boys. They were there by themselves, with just the dragons. He figured they would have to clean the stables for a week for their latest stunt.

Now, do ye understand? Westerly, Westerly, did ye hear anything Ay just told ye? said Báncliete.

I'm sorry. Did you say something?

Riley, Ay'm going to hae to connect him with the falcon.

I thought we decided he would try something close by first, said Riley. *Báncliete, this might not be a good idea.*

The wee anes are missing. Things hae cheenged.

Are you saying there is something I can do to help find the girls? If there is, I want to try, said Westerly.

Westerly, you must promise to do exactly as Báncliete says, said Riley.

Westerly nodded his agreement. Then he walked over to a chair with only a thin cushion on it. He sat down. Then he stood up and moved the chair so it was exactly in the center of the map.

Báncliete told him to ask the map where the falcon was right now. The map moved around and a small object that could have been a falcon, but looked more like a sparrow, appeared. Then the map changed as it showed more details of where the falcon was flying. Báncliete suggested to Westerly that he find the most comfortable place in the room and either sit or lie down. Westerly shoved the chair aside and pulled over several large over stuffed pillows. One he placed against the bed and the other he sat down cross-legged and leaned back.

Now, what I need you to do is close your eyes. Picture the falcon and the area where the map said he was, said Riley.

Got it.

Good, you know how you are working on talking to the others through your minds. What you're going to do is ask the falcon to let you into his mind. Ask him if you can fly with him.

How? I don't know his language.

For a moment, there was a silence that filled the room. Then the songs of the birds crept in from the windows. Westerly started humming along.

What I think you should do is sing to the falcon. Tell him in music what you would like. While you're singing, picture the land around where the falcon is flying, said Riley.

Westerly didn't answer them. He began singing to the falcon. He told the bird of the missing girls and how much Siona meant to him. Westerly told the bird about teaching Siona the ways of the woods and with pride, he explained how quickly she learned. Then he sang about meeting with the ancient oak and how it was her idea to ask the totems to help locate the girls.

Please, great falcon, let me see through your eyes so I might seek the evil that took the children, said Westerly.

Westerly could feel a shift in how he saw the land. It was dazzling. There appeared to be more colors, more definition. He could see details he had never noticed before, and he knew he was seeing through the bird's-eye. Westerly noticed a group that was traveling slowly and he sang to the falcon, asking it to go closer to the group. As the falcon dove toward the travelers, Westerly could clearly make out Tristan's features. He saw how tense his face was and the anguish in his friend's eyes.

You need to let the falcon go. It's time to come back to your room. Sing your goodbyes. Use the come home song you sing for Aine and Brydon, said Riley.

There was resistance from Westerly, and it worried the essences. Just as they thought to call for help, Farah and Dalton walked in. They stopped short when they saw that Westerly's eyes were almond shaped and the same dark black of the Falcon's.

Farah, Westerly is off with the falcon. He needs to come back. Can you sing one of the call and response songs? He needs to rejoin us before he becomes lost in the falcon, said Riley.

Dalton looked at Farah, and she nodded to him. He pulled out a wind stick and began playing a tune that the essences had not heard before. Farah's clear voice began a song that she, Dalton and Westerly had written on their trip to the elf palace over the summer. It started off by asking if the elf king would let a dwarf come to the palace. Then it described their journey. It told of the woods they traveled through and asked Westerly to describe them. When he didn't answer, Farah's voice faltered. Dalton took up the song demanding that Westerly assure Farah that they would accept her at court even though she was only half-elf. Still, there was no answer. Then the door opened, and the others came in.

Farah took the song back and pleaded with Westerly to answer. While she did this, Dalton explained what had happened to the others.

He's not grounded, and he isn't wearing his touchstone, said Aine. *Westerly grounds Brydon and I when we leave our bodies. He needs someone to ground him.*

While the others exchanged looks, Mirah walked to the dressing table and picked up Westerly's touchstone. She walked over to him and placed it around his neck, then stood to one side and placed a hand on his shoulder. She nodded to Barra, who went and grasped his other shoulder. Then, with her free hand, she waved to Farah, who stopped singing. Though Mirah didn't have the complex tones that came from Farah, her voice was that of spring, with new growth springing from the ground. She sang to Westerly of the falcons and what they saw. Then of the nest they returned to so they could be with their mate and chicks. Finally she sang of the falcon totem. The importance of it looking over all of them. Of the need for it to guard the hall of the guides. She asked the falcon totem to come home and bring Westerly with him. Barra dug into Westerly's shoulder, causing pain. They had learned that pain could help clear the mind. Slowly, like he was relearning how to speak, Westerly answered Mirah's song. He told her of the totems' regret of not being asked to fly, that it had missed spreading its wings. Mirah agreed it would be sad and assured the totem that wouldn't happen again. It would fly often, now that they understood its need. He just needed to bring Westerly back to them.

As the conversation wound down, Barra increased the pressure on Westerly. She kept it up until he shrugged his shoulder, turned his head and glared at her. Once she saw his eyes return to their normal shape, she let go. As she did, Westerly tumbled forward. Before the others could even blink, Barra had him in her arms and was placing him on the bed.

Thank you. I was so caught up in being the falcon, I forgot who I was.

Missing girls or not, we need to take this slower or we will lose you, said Riley.

"What did your essences tell you?" asked Farah.

20

Chapter 20—Escape Plan

Siona's stomach growled, and she thought about how wonderful her adopted mother's cooking was. She missed helping make bread. She missed the smell of bacon sizzling and cracking eggs to cook. Siona missed her new father, Cadryn, as he read to her and told stories of the old times, telling her she was very smart and would soon join the others at the school. She even missed her brothers.

She thought about the times before her new family, when Tristan had to beg the villagers for food. She knew he always waited to eat last to make sure she and Ryuu had enough. Siona thought about Ryuu and how, back in their village, he never let the other boys tease her, even though he did it himself. She thought about her new brothers and sister, how happy they were to have them as part of the family. Siona wondered, did they miss her? She had overheard Mirah, her new sister, tell her twin Brydon that their mother didn't know it, but the family was going to grow again, she was going to have another baby.

Mirah knew things without learning, stuff about people and animals. She knew how to help women have births and be safe. Some said she was better than the midwives. Brydon was on the other side, the dark as she thought of it. He talked to spirits and the ones who lived in the forest's darkness. Sometimes she thought it was creepy, but they and Tristan were special. They were part of the Guides, who she knew would someday fight to save the kingdom. Siona wished she was special, too. But right now, all she wanted was to go home and be with her family. She was tired of this cave and tired of being afraid. Tears trickled down her face.

The old man looked over and saw her tears. For a second, it looked like he was sorry for her, but then he left the cave. She wondered if he regretted what he said to his granddaughter.

Banprionsa looked over at Siona and shouted into her mind, *Somebodie will rescue hus soon! Thay are looking for hus and ye ken thay will n'er stop until thay find hus.*

Like a whisper of the wind, Siona said, *We will...I just want to go home. I miss everyone.*

Ay miss my faither too. What do ye want to do? asked Banprionsa.

He hurt me. She said, rubbing her skin, as if to assure herself it was still there. *We still need to keep trying to escape or he will kill you.*

Ye need to stop crying. We'll figure sommit out. D'noo forget, Ay'm harder to kill than ye realize.

At this, Siona moved closer and leaned on Banprionsa. She turned her head and Banprionsa awkwardly worked a wing around her so the girls were as close as they could be. After crying for a bit more, Siona fell back into an exhausted sleep.

The old man reentered the cave after he had searched the area for signs of his enemy. From what Tegan had said, they couldn't be far off. He knew he needed to feed the girls... no, captives. He looked around and only saw the dragon.

Where's Siona? How did she get away this time? Doesn't she realize what I will do when I find her? Wasn't that enough of a...

Banprionsa hissed. *Noo so loud. She is sleeping. The fire went out, and she got cold. She is under my wing to get warm.*

Let me see.

Banprionsa moved her wing just enough so he could see Siona curled up against her. He noticed that her long hair wasn't tucked all the way inside the wing.

You two are usually chattering like the songbirds by now. What's wrong with her?

What do ye think is wrong with her? Ye terrified her with that trick ye did. Is she supposed to just laugh and carry on?

She got what she deserved and it will be worse next time.

Don't ye realize she's homesick and wants her faimlie? Do ye really need both of us? Let Siona ga and just keep me.

No.

Yer stupid spell did some damage. She's getting sick. Do ye want to deal with a sick wee ane?

If she gets sick, she gets sick. If she dies, well, that's just the way it is.

Yer granddochter will noo be happy if she dies.

You know nothing about Te... her. I don't have a granddaughter anymore.

She bonded to a dragon. Ay can smell it.

At that, the old man dropped a plate of cold rabbit, cheese and bread in front of Banprionsa. Then he stomped out of the cavern. As he turned, Banprionsa saw a look run across his face. Guilt? Sorrow? Human's limited color vocabulary made them difficult to read. As she watched him leave red-faced, she knew she had gotten under his skin. She smiled and thought maybe this would make him careless. She felt Siona moving under her wing and she pulled it open and saw that Siona was grinning at her.

You got to him; I think.

He's gaen for a while, said Banprionsa. Ay hae an idea of how ye might escape undetected, at least for a while.

Really. What is it?

So Banprionsa formed pictures for Siona in her mind. She showed Siona, the old man coming into the cave. He would look over and not see Siona then do precisely what he did today, which was walk over to them and see the hair. Banprionsa, when asked, would pull back the wing and he would see Siona sleeping under her arm with just a piece of braid showing. Every once in a while, Siona needed to make sounds like she was sobbing.

He thinks ye are upset. As long as he sees your hair, he willnae ask after the first couple of times.

But when I leave, he will no longer see the hair.

Ye won't like this part of the idea.

I won't like what?

We need a knife. Ye will have to cut off your hair. That way, after ye leave, your braid will still show.

You want me to...

Get under; he's coming.

Banprionsa's sharp ears allowed her to hear the first scrape of the old man's shoe as he entered the cave. Before he got to the back, Siona was neatly tucked under Banprionsa's wing, with a bit of her braid showing. She pretended to sob loud enough that the old man would hear them. She was an accomplished fake-crier as she used it with her brothers when she wanted to get her way. The old man just looked at the girls and then exited the cave again. Banprionsa moved her wing and looked at Siona. She smiled.

I'm tired. Mind if I stay under here and sleep for a while?

As an answer, Banprionsa folded her wing down over Siona and both girls fell asleep and dreamed. While they slept, their dreams merged like flashes: the first time they discovered they were connected, Siona, through Banprionsa's images, relived her first flight, the sorrow that Siona felt after losing her parents to bandits. They provided each other comfort through the years, long before they meet in person. When they were connected, and spoke, their thoughts had spanned the hundreds of miles that separated them. Then came their actual meeting and now they both ended up prisoners. As this thought came to them, they stirred and awakened.

Siona reacted first, and Banprionsa quickly raised her wing. She sat up and looked around. The old man was still not back.

Do you think I can leave tomorrow?

Ay think we best wait one more day.

The girls spent the rest of the day discussing their families and wondering what they were doing to find them. They never doubted for a moment that searchers were out looking. But they knew that powerful magic surrounded this place, like lichen-covered a tree trunk. Unless you were right on top of it, you would never know that it was there.

He's comin.

Siona dodged under Banprionsa's wing and made small hiccuping noises, as if she had just stopped crying. The old man grunted. He fixed dinner, took his and went outside to enjoy the stars and not have to hear Siona's sounds of sorrow. The next day went like the first, except the old man did not ask to see Siona. As long as he saw her hair, he assumed she was there.

On the third day, after the old man left their breakfast, Siona came out from under Banprionsa's wing. She reached back behind her, grabbed her hair and sawed it off. It was a good thing that he never realized she had taken a knife the first time she wandered the cavern. She had tucked it behind Banprionsa and there it had stayed safely out of sight. The knife was very sharp, and it only took a few cuts before the braid came off. She smiled and put a knot on the other end and then secured it to one of Banprionsa's scales. As long as Banprionsa didn't move too much, it would work out fine. Though she put on a brave front, Banprionsa was worried about what Siona might encounter once left the cave.

Are ye ready?

Yes, but are you sure he won't hurt you?

Ay am harder to hurt. Ay will take the chance.

Siona threw her arms around Banprionsa's neck and hugged as hard as she could. The girls looked at each other and then Siona stood. She went over to the table, grabbed some fruit and a few slices of bread, hoping the old man wouldn't notice. She turned, smiled at her friend, and walked toward the cave entrance without looking back. As soon as she got to the mouth of the cave, she poked her head out to make sure he wasn't nearby. When Siona didn't see him, she ran towards the woods for cover.

21

Chapter 21—The Woods

As Siona darted forward, she saw a path and sprinted toward it. She thought she heard a voice telling her *not that path.* But it couldn't be, it was just the sound of the wind. When she came to the trail and took a step, the trees bent and blocked her way. She thought she felt a hand pushing her further south. Is this what Brydon meant when he said the woods talk to him? She wondered though, who controlled them? Were they helping or herding her for the old man? Siona worried. What choice did she have but to use the woods for escape?

A second time, she started into the woods and had her way obstructed. Again, she felt as if she was being maneuvered to a specific place. On her third try, she found a small path that looked as if it hadn't been trod on in a long time. Saplings sprouted in it and boulders pushed up from the earth, but at least for now she could step over them. On one side was a stream of murky brown water that reminded her of dried blood. On the other was a wall of brambles that, if she got too close, would tear her skin. Among the bushes, she spotted dark fruit that looked like blackberries. It tempted her to pick one, but was afraid the thorns would cut her. Maybe if she ran out of food, she would try them.

As Siona moved along the path, she brushed against the bushes and felt something grab her. She looked down and found that a vine had entwined her wrist. It was pulling her toward the spiked barrier. When she looked, Siona saw skeletons of small animals among the roots. She tried frantically to pull loose, but it tightened with each effort. Siona remembered hearing plucking a leaf could hurt a plant. So, she reached over and pulled a leaf off.

"Let go of me or I will pull all of your leaves off."

Even though she felt silly talking to the plant, Siona was getting desperate. Realizing that its hold had lessened, she ripped her hand free. She saw a few drops of blood trickled down her hand. She wiped it on her shirt then continued down the path, sometimes scrambling over boulders, intermittently having to wade in the vile-looking stream.

She came to a bend in the trail and again the trees blocked her. But this time it was different. Siona heard crashing, then silence. After a moment, she heard soft crunching sounds like something large coming towards her. Stalking her.

"Who's there?"

But instead of a voice, what she heard was a low growl, like a wild beast scant inches from her, just on the other side the brambles. Sweat trickled down her forehead and into her eyes. She looked for a place to run, but her feet were more firmly rooted than the forest itself. Siona didn't know what to do or where to go. Instead of moving, she looked around, trying to find anywhere to hide. Again, she thought she heard a voice.

"Climb the tree to your right."

"Who's there? Answer me. What do you want?"

"Climb, now!"

Again, she heard a growl, and it seemed closer. Suddenly, the voice, which must be in her head, made sense. She scrambled to the tree and went to the first limb, which overhung the water. There was a loud crack, and the branch shifted downward under her weight.

"This can't be a good idea."

"Go higher!"

"Who are you?"

But even as she asked, Siona climbed several branches higher until she could just see over the top of the bushes to what was stalking her. There was a giant wolf, twice the size of any she had seen before and ten times as frightening. Its auburn fur was sticking straight up as if it were on high alert. It moved back several feet, ran and cleared the top of the barrier with room to spare.

As it landed, she confirmed just how big it was. Standing on four legs, it was taller than she was on two. The paws were the size of dinner plates. The wolf looked around, its head up, sniffing until it caught her scent. It looked up at her with greedy glowing golden eyes that seem to bore into her soul. The wolf stalked over to the tree, circling it several times. He stopping once or twice to test a perch, searching with pitiless orbs, for a way to reach her. It took several steps back, ran, jumped on to a nearby branch, swiping its huge paws at her. It caught the sleeve of her shirt, but not her skin.

Carried by its own weight, the wolf tumbled back to the ground. Even as he dropped, his burning gaze never shifted from her. Siona clambered further up the tree, wanting to be as far away from the wolf as she could. She was ecstatic knowing the wolf could jump on to a branch, but not actually climb the tree. Siona was confident, sort of, that if the beast got to a branch, it wouldn't be able to hold his weight.

"Hold on."

Even as those instructions rang through her mind, Siona had already wrapped her arms and legs around the tree limb, like a baby opossum clinging for life to its mother. She snuggled as close to the trunk as she could, so it wedged her in tight. Siona watched the wolf as it backed away and again ran at the tree, but instead of jumping, it rammed into the trunk, causing the whole thing to sway. The creature backed up and did it once, twice more. She heard and felt the tree groan under her grasp. Then, to her astonishment, the surrounding trees moved and swatted at the wolf. She felt a laugh stick in her throat, too afraid to come out. The brambles untangled and reached for a leg, grabbed it and dug in. The wolf yowled in surprise, pain and anger. Siona thought she could see blood. The wolf turned toward what seized his leg and, whining with pain, chewed on it until he was free. Bleeding from his thorn torn mouth, he fled down the path at a fast trot, pausing only to glare back at her with frustrated malevolence. Siona started to climb down out of the tree when, again, the voice sounded in her ear.

"Stay."

After what had just happened, she did what the voice said. So far, it had not failed her. But she wondered who it was and why it sounded like the wind. Each time the voice had come, it felt like feathers tickling her ear as a warm breeze brushed over her cheek. Again, she heard a noise and looked around. It was the old man. *No, he couldn't be heading back so soon. Would he find she was missing?* As those thoughts entered her head, she realized he wasn't going toward the cave, but away from it. Siona gave a silent prayer to the goddesses and hoped they, or whoever it was, would keep watching over her. From her perch, she could hear the old man muttering.

"Damn that wolf; I told him to watch for intruders and to keep them for me. Why did it have to eat that deer I trapped? I wanted something besides a rabbit to eat. Now I've got to go find him and figure out what to do. I can't let him wander the mountains if he doesn't follow my instructions."

Siona was stunned that he kept this giant like a guard dog. Who would do something like that? Wasn't he afraid it would turn on him? Maybe that would be a good thing. She hoped the old man banished the wolf. She didn't want to run into it again. Siona stayed in the tree for the rest of the day, and just as dusk came, she saw the old man return. After he had passed by, she began to climb down.

"Stay here. Sleep."

With that, Siona felt her eyes involuntarily grow heavy, and she closed them. The branches reached down and cradled her, making a warm bed so snug so she would be safe for the night.

22

Chapter 22—Return to Ashwind

Tegan flew like a falcon toward the castle. She was eager to get back and spend time with her dragon, Gearcleite. Maybe they could even ride. How different would the wind feel, soaring through the air like an eagle? Would it be the same as riding on her horse? Coming closer to the campsite of the searchers, Tegan knew she would have to stop briefly. Did they know about her grandfather? She smelled their fire, rabbit stew and that hot bitter brown brew adults liked so much.

Tegan reined in her horse upon entering their camp. Ainmire was stirring the pot of stew and the three dragons had their backs to the fire. It looked like they were eating. She had seen grandfather's wild wolf do that same thing. Turn away to hide its food from the sight of others, almost as if they feared it would be taken. Two of the dragons must be adults. They were much more massive than Gearcleite. Tegan wondered how hard it was going to be to get on her dragon. How did they mount these that were so much larger? She could hear her grandfather in her head, telling her it just took practice.

"Tegan, I see you got permission to go back to the castle," said Ainmire.

"Yes sir, I did. Have you found any signs of the missing ones?"

"Not yet, but we will keep looking. Would you like some breakfast?"

"No, thanks. I need to get going or I might be late."

"Wait just a moment. Conall, is the scroll ready?"

At that, Conall walked up, blowing on some wax affixed to a piece of parchment. He looked as if he wanted to speak, but just handed it to Ainmire and walked back to the fire. Ainmire knew he wasn't sure that they should send this to the Guardian, but they had decided it needed to be done.

"Would you deliver this to the Guardian as soon as you arrive?"

"Yes. What's in it?"

Ainmire looked Tegan in the eye and wondered for one moment about why she would ask. Then he flashed to his students and decided it was just childish curiosity.

"Nothing exciting. Just telling the Guardian that we have found nothing."

"I need to go now. But I'll see he gets it. Good luck."

Do ye think she will read it? asked Banríoncruba.

"I'm not sure."

Ainmire thought first of his niece, Aine, then of the Guides. Would they look? The warriors would look. They'd justify it by saying it was their job to protect. The others would try to find another way to know what was being said. They'd try to listen in when they looked like they were doing chores. That always made him smile. They thought they were so slick, coming in, pretending they were doing a job that wasn't theirs to do just to find out what he and Ferris or Cadryn were talking about.

He knew he had responsibilities to the school, but the missing ones took precedence over all of that for the moment. There were other outstanding teachers that would go on without him for several more weeks if it came to that. There were plans for the next two months out, but they were always adjusting things, depending on what happened.

Dragons arriving. That would take adjustments. He knew Cadryn would talk things over with Ferris and come up with a plan. Ainmire just felt a little guilty about not be there to help. He was also worried about Aine. He wondered what the king would say that his heir had bonded with a dragon. Hopefully, he would remember the old stories and that past rulers had bonded. Nothing could be done about it now. She was bonded and nothing he could do would change that.

Tegan secured the scroll, kicked her horse and shot off again as if a fire were chasing her. *I wonder if he really told me what was in the scroll. Should I open it? No, I'll never get the wax on right again. Maybe I'll listen in while the Guardian reads it.*

She galloped for hours, never stopping to admire the passing scenery. Tegan barely noticed the warren of rabbits or the stag grazing in a meadow with his doe. She didn't see the bluebells that were just popping up out of the soil. All her thoughts bounced between Ashwind and her grandfather.

With her mount breathing hard, she entered the courtyard. Tegan saw the Guardian across the way, dismounted and headed toward him. She pulled out the scroll and waited to be acknowledged. She had learned from her grandfather that interrupting wasn't a good idea.

"Tegan, you've returned. Very glad to see you. Take your horse to the stables and ask the groom to take care of it for you. Then come back here."

"Please sir, the people searching asked me to give this to you."

At that, she presented him with the parchment and pretended to walk away. The Guardian saw Conall's seal. *What did he have to say that he couldn't send through his dragon?* He stepped away from the group and read it.

"Old friend, I think your brother lives and it is he who captured the girls. Someone who can levitate large objects moved Banprionsa and I've only met one person who could do this. I'm sorry, but I believe it is him." The Guardian blinked and reread the message. He shut his eyes for a moment and saw them all as they once had been: young, happy and free. The Guardian called out to Tegan, and she turned to face him. Stunned, he paused for a moment, collecting his thoughts.

"Tegan, did you get breakfast?"

"No, but I'm fine."

"Go see Emmair and she will give you at least some bread and cheese."

Yes, he could see it now. How had he not known? She had his green eyes and smiled just like he did, as if he knew a great secret. That wonderful young girl was related to him. A niece or great-niece? What was he going to do now? Did she know where his brother, Garvin, was hiding? What should he do, call her back and confront her? Was she part of his plan? Did she have brothers and sisters? Was her aunt even real? No, she had told as much of the truth as she felt she could. He didn't think Tegan knew they were related. He would tell Dubhbragh and together they'd decide what to do. The Guardian hoped this child wouldn't get caught up in the fight that was sure to come. Whatever happened, Tegan was as innocent as the two who were being held captive.

The Guardian's feelings were mixed. He was sad that Garvin had taken the girls. He really wanted his brother back. They had been such great friends as boys, and he knew he had let his authority overrule his love and had shoved Garvin and Conall away. He knew that if he had taken the time to listen and consider, even discuss with them what they had seen, they might not have gone to the other side. But in his arrogance, he had told them they were wrong. Truth, the Guardian had not searched hard for his brother. He had been afraid they would put Garvin to death. He could not be responsible for that happening.

Tegan walked toward the stables, confused by the look that she had seen on the Guardian's face, as if he recognized her. How could he? He thought her Grandfather dead, so he should not even think about him. But she remembered the old man's warning and Tegan planned to stay clear of him as much as she could. Tegan was saddened by how she and her grandfather had parted. She loved him more than anyone else.

Tegan thought he wouldn't stay angry. He hadn't before. She would do what she had planned, mingle with the other kids and their dragons. Make friends. That was what she had told her grandfather. It was the best way not to be noticed. Tegan knew people tell their friends things they don't divulge to others. She needed to collect information; she still thought that was her job and she would do it. Tegan was just about at the stables when an elf girl and a human boy approached her.

"Are you Tegan?" said Brydon.

"Yes."

"Oh good, I am Brydon and this is Aine. My mom's Emmair and she sent me to get you."

"I really am not hungry."

"You don't want to get me in trouble. If I do not come back with you, my mom will not be happy with me," said Brydon.

"You might as well come back with us. Emmair will just come and find you herself," said Aine.

"She will?"

"She's done it to us more than once," said Aine.

Tegan handed her horse off to the groom, who promised to give it a good rub and extra oats. At that, Tegan followed Brydon and Aine to where Emmair stood outside the front door of the largest house she had ever seen. Emmair ushered her in and the other two followed, hoping for a second breakfast. There on the table before her was what she thought of as a feast. Freshly made bread, large slices of ham that still sizzled as if it had come right off the stove, scrambled eggs that looked kind of orange as if cheese were in them. There were strawberries and cream. Despite herself, her mouth watered and her stomach rumbled, which would have given her away if she said she wasn't hungry.

"I thought I was to get bread and cheese."

"Nonsense, you had a long ride and I dare say didn't eat before you left. Eat now!" said Emmair.

"Mum."

"Hadn't you two just eaten? Well, go on. You can keep Tegan company while I do some cleaning."

With that, Emmair left the three children on their own. At first, the only sound was that of forks hitting plates as they ate their fill in the silence. Tegan kept glancing up at the other two and couldn't help but feel guilty. She knew the girl taken was Emmair's adopted daughter. Why did her grandfather need her? These people seemed so nice, and she hoped she could keep her counsel and not let anything slip. If her grandfather came to harm because of her, she would never forgive herself. She also knew that sitting here quietly wouldn't make her friends. She needed to show an interest in what was happening. Everybody was talking about the missing girl and dragon, so Tegan decided she should ask.

"I know someone is missing. I met the searchers. Can I ask, do you know what happened?"

Brydon's fork hit the table, and the laughter died from his eyes. He looked at Tegan and tried to speak, but no words came out. He cleared his throat and still couldn't talk. Aine reached under the table and squeezed his hand.

"The girl who was missing is Siona. She's Brydon's sister. She didn't go missing. Someone took her."

"Really, how?"

"We don't know. If you're done eating, we should join the others."

The three got up from the table and Tegan automatically picked up her plate and took it to the sink. She reached for the other's dishes and then around for the washing cloth.

"Leave it. Mum said she would do them today," said Brydon.

As they left, Tegan peppered them with questions about the school and what they would learn. She asked how much time they got to spend with the dragons. Had they been able to ride? She laughed at the description that Brydon gave her of Pogee trying to climb up on his dragon and just ending up sliding down, landing on his rump. There was an easy camaraderie between the three by the time they made it to the training area. As soon as they arrived, Tegan broke off to find Gearcleite. She waved goodbye and walked to the other side.

Nessa had been standing in the shadow of the castle wall, watching for Tegan. She had her orders to make friends with the girl. This could be hard, as Nessa preferred the company of boys and stuck close to her cousin, Carin. But this was important, and they were on a mission. If they could cause enough strife, Nessa and the others believed that the subhuman dwarves and elves would go back to where they belonged. It was horrible to pretend to make friends with these creatures. Especially Aine, who acted as if she was as good as a person. She needed to be taught her place.

A few moments later, Tegan glanced over her shoulder and saw a girl catching up to her. She wondered why, but slowed so she could find out.

Nessa's thoughts were like a whirlwind. *I need to find out if Tegan was an agent of the Old Man. Or if she just got here by chance and knew nothing.* Nessa was part of the group working with Tegan's grandfather. She was the one who lured Siona away. Before Tegan asked her too many questions, Nessa thought to herself, *I need to make friends with her*. Nessa knew it would be much easier to communicate with the Old Man if Tegan could do it for them. As Nessa approached, she affected a smile. She had a quick, friendly smile, though she rarely shared it with anyone outside of her circle.

"I'm Nessa. Is that the dragon that bonded with you?"

"Yes, are you bonded with one, too?" asked Tegan.

"The one right next to yours."

"Have you gotten to ride yet?"

"Not yet. When nobody was looking, I climbed on top of him. I hope it's today. I'm Nessa."

"Hi, I'm Tegan."

When they got close to the dragons, Nessa couldn't help herself. She needed to spend time with Donncruba. She could feel the questions coming out of the dragon. Her dragon wondered why she waited so long to come over. Nessa formed a picture in her mind of wanting to make friends with the new girl. Showing her the boys she had as friends and letting her know she wished she had a girl for a friend.

"Talk to you in a few minutes. I want to spend time with Donncruba."

Tegan was happy the other girl had left. All she wanted was to learn about her dragon. She still needed to learn her name. As if the thought had directly gone to the dragon. Tegan heard in her mind. *I am Gearcleite. I think you are Tegan.*

Tegan nodded her head yes. She walked over and placed her head on Gearcleite's neck.

23

Chapter 23 — Flying Lessons

After they greeted each other, Gearcleite made word pictures showing Tegan riding her horse. There was a question in them that Tegan picked up on.

The scales of the dragon's breast glowed with an unfamiliar sunflower color she couldn't interpret. Tegan tried to just talk with her mind, but found it difficult, so she spoke the words out loud. She shared her excitement to be bonded with the dragon and hoped being experienced at horseback riding would help her be able to ride with Gearcleite better. She talked about the picture she had formed of her flying over the cliffs and how Tegan wanted to see the world from a vantage point that she could only get by being with Gearcleite. At that, the dragon seemed satisfied. The envious yellow faded from her scales. She didn't want to be second to a horse. Gearcleite knew horses couldn't communicate the way dragons did. She still felt jealous of Tegan's love for her mare.

Do you think we'll get to ride together today? said Tegan.

Ay sure hope so. Ay wants ye to see the world as Ay do, said Gearcleite.

"Tegan, they're waving at us to join them. Come on, let's see if we can stay near each other," said Nessa.

Tegan agreed, though there was something about Nessa being friendly that seemed forced. She felt more comfortable with Brydon and Aine. Tegan spotted them and they were waving to her. She turned to Nessa and suggested they join them. Nessa looked uncomfortable, but agreed. Both of them were thinking about how they needed to be friends and gather information; each, though, had their own reasons. As they went to join Brydon and Aine, both of them noticed the Guardian was leaving.

"Hi, you two. Either of you know where the Guardian is going? I thought he was giving lessons this morning," said Nessa.

"I do not know, but I can guess," said Brydon.

"Oh, what's your guess?" said Tegan.

"I think he is going to go see the searchers and talk to him in person. I overheard him tell my mum last night that he might do that."

Tegan breathed a sigh of relief. If he had planned this last night, it wouldn't have anything to do with the scroll she brought. She was worried. What if he found her grandfather? What would happen? Her heart hurt. Her face reflected the worry Tegan felt; she looked down, hoping nobody had noticed.

"Tegan, are you all right? You look worried," said Aine.

"No, just disappointed. I guess we won't be riding today."

Just then, an adult stood up and raised his arm, waiting for everyone to look his way and pay attention. Then Ferris smiled at them and asked the group to separate into those who had ridden horses and those who had not. Aine and Tegan joined the group that had, leaving Brydon and Nessa in the other group.

"See you later," said Aine.

"Let's meet for lunch and share what happened," said Brydon.

Aine and Tegan hurriedly joined the smaller group. She kept giving Tegan a sidelong look.

"Aine, is there something wrong?"

"I was just surprised to see you with Nessa."

"Why?"

"I didn't know you knew anybody here."

"I don't. The first kids I meet were you and Brydon. She came up to me as I was walking over to Gearcleite."

"I don't know Nessa well. She almost always stays with her small group of friends, mostly boys. It might be nice if we both got to know her better."

Maybe the fact that she spent time with boys was why she seemed off. It could be she just wanted a girlfriend, but didn't know how to go about making one. Tegan knew how that felt; she spent so much time with her grandfather she felt shy around other people, especially those of her own age. They walked over and joined their group.

"That's Ferris up front. We better pay attention."

At that, Ferris announced that those who could mount their dragons would get to fly. But only close to the ground until they got the hang of it. Tegan and Aine exchanged looks of excitement. They were going to fly.

24

Chapter 24—Banprionsa's Worry

Banprionsa awakened abruptly from her dream. She lifted her head just enough to look around. She hoped he did not notice her movements. By the single candle burning in the cave, she saw the old man moving around collecting gear. As Banprionsa tracked him under lidded eyes, she decided he gathered his hunting gear so he could go for large animals. This was the first time she had seen him grab the great bow that had hung to the left of the cooking fire. He gathered a stack of arrows with unusually stout shafts, nearly the length of a man's leg. He inspected each one, tossing aside those that he didn't put into his quiver. She wondered what he was hunting and said a prayer to the Gods: it wasn't Siona. At the thought of Siona, she shuddered. Banprionsa watched as the old man as he finished gathering his things and, without even a backward glance at her, strode from the cave.

Banprionsa had noticed things she hadn't when Siona was with her. She observed that the curtain, used to keep the bathing area separate, was comprised of grain sacks of coarse fiber. The old man had collected and stitched together enough sacks to cover the opening. There was a board used for cutting meats and vegetables. There were pit marks from age and constant use. Soot and scorch marks covered the pots and pans, giving them an aged appearance and making it impossible to determine their material. Only the knives looked well cared for. The steel gleamed, and they had finely made the handles. Banprionsa thought they were deer antlers. Each had its own sheath made of leather that he placed them back into after use. She wondered at their different purposes and where they could have come from. They were not like what she had seen before. She wished Siona was there to share her thoughts in the early morning.

Now that she was wide awake, Banprionsa could not help but wonder where Siona was and if she was safe. She sent her thoughts out, searching for her with little hope she would hear. Banprionsa sat there feeling as if she was all alone in the world. Cut off from Siona, as if she was actually dead. No second voice in her head teasing her mind, making her laugh. Banprionsa let out a sigh as a tear ran down her chitin-plated cheek. She could not live like this if he killed Siona. She understood now why they said dragons and their riders died soon after each other. The loss was more than anything she had ever felt before. This was not something she had thought of.

Banprionsa lifted her head, turning it slightly as if she heard something. She felt a breeze that she had never sensed inside the cave. There it was again. A breeze, like a feather, which touched her face. But there was more; she shut her thoughts off so she could concentrate on what was happening. There were words on the wind.

Siona is fine. She slept through the night as we watched over her.

Who are ye?

Banprionsa, all you need to know is we are friends watching out for Siona.

The old man has a weapon. Is he...

No, he doesn't know about her yet. We have duties elsewhere. We will come back if we can.

Banprionsa thought, *Wait,* but she knew it was too late. Once again, she was all by herself.

She was tired of sitting on this floor, shifting around to keep the rocks from digging too deep into any one part of her. The shot of joy at knowing Siona was fine faded quickly, and Banprionsa descended again into loneliness. When you always had someone in your head, this quiet was difficult to tolerate. A part of you was missing. She and Siona had been together since their birth date, having found each other in the ether before being born. That was when they joined and never a day had passed when they hadn't felt the other's essence inside. Now, Siona's spirit was missing; it was as if a part of her soul had fled. She hoped Siona would find help soon before this numbness consumed her.

25

Chapter 25—The Wolf

Siona moved around when the wind came to her again.

"He's coming."

At that, Siona stopped stretching and went on high alert. Even as she did, she tossed her thoughts to Banprionsa, knowing she might not hear her. But she had to try; she felt a part of her was missing. As the old man strode by, she noticed he was carrying a bow, enormous enough to kill something large. As that thought formed, she remembered he had said he needed to do something about the wolf. *Was this what he was going to do, kill that magnificent animal for eating his stupid deer? Didn't he know that was what they did?* He wanted the wolf to act contrary to its nature.

Siona loved all animals, from the time she could walk. Whenever there was an animal hurt, she had tried to save it. Mostly they had been small animals, birds, squirrels, or even the village stray cats. Before her death, she learned a lot from her mother about healing plants. After that, she learned from trial and error. The first time Mirah, her new sister, brought home a sick animal, she was excited. Then Mirah had let her take over, much to her new family's surprise, and made sure that the little dog had not just gotten well, but had thrived. They had given her a room, really a shed, where she could keep her tools and the animals would be safe while they recovered. Siona wondered if she could save the wolf and climbed down.

"Not yet. Stay."

"But he is going to kill the wolf. I can't let that happen."

"He will try, but we will help the wolf if you stay."

Siona nodded her assent, even though there was nobody to see her, and settled back just as her stomach grumbled. Within a minute, a leaf ascended to her level and stopped within, easy reach uncurled itself, revealing the fruit it bore. There was the black fruit she had seen yesterday, and a round fruit that looked familiar, except it was the color of fresh-cut grass. Put off by the green hue, she reached for the black fruit and ate it. The juice was so sweet she put several in her mouth at once. She bit down and deep purple sprayed from between her lips and ran down her chin. She smiled at that, then wiped her face with the back of her sleeve, which was brown now from days sleeping in the cave. Siona picked up the green fruit and turned it over. It looked the same shape, size and texture as the red fruit she ate at home...but the color. She took a small bite and chewed once, then spit it out. It was tart like the yellow fruit they made juice out of. There was something she liked, so she tried again, chewing it slowly and letting the nectar trickle down her throat. She then took her third bite and kept eating it until she was down to the core. She placed it on the leaf plate and watched as it curled around the leftovers and moved away from her.

Siona thought of going to drink from the stream, when once again the leaf was there. It uncurled and revealed the most enormous acorn she had ever seen, brimming with water. As the cool water soothed her dry mouth, she sipped it and knew it was from the creek. She liked the nutty flavor that the cup had added to the water. She would remember this and tell the others how it added a dimension that was missing with just plain water. As she watched her cup descend, she heard whistling: the old man was near. She coiled as close to the branch as she could so she would be as small as possible in case he looked up. As he strode by, she thought he had fewer arrows than before. She could hear him mutter.

"I would have finished him if he hadn't run into the forest. Not sure how he disappeared so fast or why I couldn't follow him. I must really be getting old. Still, he should bleed out, with what I hit him with."

Siona had to catch herself from shouting at the old man. She must have made some sound, for he stopped and looked around. The limbs shifted slightly, so even as he glanced up, it blocked her from his view. He moved on after checking all around. He rounded the bend and then, just as Siona thought it was safe, there he was again. The wind picked up and a cool breeze blew just a little harder than it usually did.

"Feels like rain. Best go check the traps to the west before it starts or there won't be anything to eat tonight."

Siona sat for what she thought was a long time. All the while worried the wolf might die. She finally scrambled down the tree. Every time she thought she would run out of branches, another appeared until she had only a short jump to the ground.

She rushed down the path in the direction that she had seen the old man come from. She trotted until she saw the spot where he had shot the wolf. There was blood on the ground. Siona followed the blood to where it entered the old growth forest. She took one tentative step and stopped. Was she doing the right thing? Hadn't the wolf tried to hurt her? She should just move on and forget him. She took a couple of steps away from the wall of trees and stopped. Siona stood, thought about the danger and then about the gorgeous wolf. She knew that the old man had set it on her and felt that she needed to help it, no matter the cost. It was just a much larger version of the animals she had tended at home. She turned around and entered the tangled woods.

26

Chapter 26—Healing

The trail was narrow, but she could follow it, just barely. She kept her eyes open, looking for blood drops and after a while, not seeing any, she wondered if she had missed something.

"Please, can you help me find him?"

"Keep walking. There is a clearing up ahead that the wolf lies in. Hurry."

Siona sped up, and shortly she was at the edge of the clearing. She saw the wolf lying on its side. Pain radiating from its eyes. As she took a step toward him, the wolf growled.

"I need to look at your wounds. I won't hurt you."

She again took a step forward, and he growled again. The wolf tried to get up, except he was too injured and fell back down. Siona moved forward again and stood just outside the range of his claws and teeth. Even hurt, it didn't mean he wasn't dangerous.

"Can you hold him down so I can look at how to get the arrows out?"

With that, roots erupted from the earth. Brown and green loops seized the wolf and held it in place. One wrapped around its muzzle so it couldn't snap at her. Siona walked over, all the time murmuring nonsense to the wolf as if speaking to an infant. She placed a hand on the wound where the first of three arrows had sunk into the wolf's side. She knew it would hurt him to pull it out, but she didn't know of any other way.

She knew she would need bandages and herbs to stop the bleeding. When her mother was alive, she had used them for healing. The one she remembered had leaves like a fern, with yellow flowers. She knew they grew in the sun mostly, and she looked around the clearing. She was in luck; there was some right at the edge of the glade. She gathered as much as she could, although she would need water to soak it in. Usually, it needed to boil to work best, but from experience, Siona knew it would work if just soaked.

"Can you bring me water?"

Siona felt silly asking the air for things, except it seemed to work, so as long as it did, she would keep asking. While she waited for what she hoped would be water coming, she separated the flowers from the stems and leaves. She would not use the stem, but the leaves could hold the poultice tight against the wounds. Then she looked for some dead vines that were no longer attached to a plant; Siona was hoping she could get them under the wolf so she could tie it in place. Just as she finished gathering everything she needed, she saw a branch descend and in it, there was a large acorn with water. It moved back up and brought down another, repeating the process until there were five large acorns of water.

"Nobody is going to believe this when I tell them."

"Some will. Tell the elf, Ainmire. He has seen this and much more through his life."

"I will if I ever get home."

Siona put the flowers into two different acorn bowls so they could soak. She knew it was time. She went to the wolf, who, with hooded eyes, had peered at all that she did. Siona sat down by his head and stroked him behind the ears as if he were a tame puppy. All the while, she explained what she was going to do. She told him she was sorry it would hurt, but that she hoped it would save him and let him return to his family. She watched his eyes and thought she could see understanding in them. With one last stroke, she went around to the side and looked again at the three arrows. She saw one that looked like it might not be in too far in and started there. She placed one hand flat against the wolf's flank, so the arrow emerged in the V between her thumb and forefinger. With her other hand, she grasped the shaft as close to the wolf's pelt as she could. Squeezing the arrow with all her might, she pulled up as fast as she could, while pushing down with the other hand. The arrow hung-up momentarily, then released with a sound like ripping canvas. The wolf's torso went rigid, then suddenly expanded. It swelled to the point of bursting, accompanied only by the sound of in-rushing air. Siona leaned back as if he might actually burst. When it seemed the beast's chest could grow no further, its mouth opened wide as a snake mid-dinner. What emerged could not accurately be called a sound. First, there came a rumbling, deep like summer thunder. The earth vibrated in sympathy. Then the basso vibration grew in pitch and volume, swelling until the grass and nearby trees recoiled at its ferocity. The wolf raised its head and partially closed his mouth. The tone climbed higher still, a geyser of anguish. Siona clapped her hands over her ears until his lungs at last depleted. The wolf's head dropped to the ground and the mighty noise faded to a wheezing whimper.

Siona inhaled sharply through her nose and clamped her lips tight. She would need to pull a lot harder to get the other arrows out. Siona swallowed hard, wishing she had not eaten the green fruit. She let the blood run to help clean the wound.

Siona steeled herself for the next extraction. This time, she leaned further over the animal's body to get better leverage. Exploding upward, she found that the second arrow came out easily. The wolf shuddered and made a keening sound that hurt Siona inside her head. The wolf's enormous head lolled to one side and his tongue, like a great raw beef roast, rolled from his mouth. He was still breathing, although he appeared unconscious. That was good, she thought; the third arrow was deeper than the others, a lot deeper. She took a deep breath and pulled. Siona could not get the arrow to move. She got off her knees and stood. Siona knew this was going to hurt the wolf, and tears formed in her eyes. She squatted down and seized the arrow, this time with both hands. She sent out a call for help and strength to all the powers, counted to three and pulled. As she drove upward with her legs, the arrow at first stubbornly resisted, then, like a petulant child playing tug-o-war, let go suddenly. Siona flew backward, arms wind-milling for support which didn't exist. She hit the ground butt first. She regained her feet, rubbing her behind, smiling in gratitude that her brothers hadn't seen her fall.

She dusted herself off and went to work. First, she took the poultice and applied it thickly to each wound. Then she got the leaves that were soaking and placed them over the poultice. They stayed where she wanted them to.

As Siona looked up, the tangerine blush to the sky and only the tip of the sun made her realize that most of the day had passed. Some instinct told her to stay with the wolf, so she gathered more plants and set them to soaking. She would change the bandage in the morning. She found that there was fruit in the area, more of those green ones, and she ate a couple of those to stave off her hunger. As night fell, she sat by the wolf, murmuring and stroking its head until she felt sleepy. She no longer felt afraid of the wolf and curled up along its back and was soon sound asleep.

The sun cresting over the trees awoke Siona the next morning. As she moved, the wolf tracked her with his eyes. Siona thought there seemed to be less pain. She noted that the vines holding the wolf down had shifted to keep the bandages in place. They brought an acorn cup of water to her, along with berries and another green fruit. There was also a fresh addition, some walnuts. She grabbed a rock and smashed the shells, eating the nuts swiftly. She drank extensively and then carried the cup to the wolf, where she tilted it so that he could lap up water with his long red tongue. After they had both finished, Siona took off the leaves and cleaned the wounds. She put more of the healing herbs onto him and covered it back up. She knew she had to get going, but she didn't like to leave him tied up.

"How can I get the vines under him to tie the leaves in place?"

The vines that were holding him lifted the wolf just enough so she could slip the loose vine rope underneath him. As she pulled the last one around, they lowered the wolf down and the vines tied the compress in place.

"Let him go now."

The vines that had held the wolf retracted back into the ground. Siona held her breath. If he was going to attack her, now would be the time. The wolf got up and moved gingerly toward her. He walked next to her side, stopped by her hand, and licked it. She reached up and stroked its head, running her hands through the silky fur, realizing for the first time just how soft it was, like the coat of a lamb. He turned and ambled toward the woods, where he disappeared from sight.

"You need to go now. You have spent too much time here already." Came to her on the wind.

Siona wiped her eyes, gathered the poultice pack, slung it over her arm, and started back the way she had come. As she reached the main path, she looked to her right and saw golden eyes watching her. She noticed it seemed to keep her pace, but stayed out of sight. The walk was peaceful, and she listened to the sound of the running creek as if it was a lullaby inviting her to stay and rest. The pull was strong, but she kept moving. She had walked so far into the forest that the sun did not penetrate through the treetops; it was like walking at night.

Through this near-night, she could see a little sun up ahead and something in the middle of the path. Because it was so dark, she couldn't really make out what it was. Then, to her surprise, it charged toward her. It was so fast she barely had time to move out of the way. A scream caught in her throat as she saw it had two large horns on its all-black head and eyes like out-of-control fire. She stood stock-still after it went past. After a few feet, it stopped and turned. The monster saw her and stared as if willing her to stay rooted like the tree she was next to.

"What should I do?"

"There is nothing we can do to help this time."

"How come?"

There was only silence, except for the beast pawing at the ground. It was like the thing could hear her heart hammering and timed his mauling of the dirt with it. She wished it wasn't so dark. She was terrified that if she moved, the animal would charge. Maybe if she just stayed still, it would leave her alone. What choice did she have? None of the trees here could she climb and Siona knew that there was no way she could outrun this thing. She heard the rustling of leaves behind her. She didn't dare take her eyes off the animal in front of her, but now whatever was behind her could attack?

"I'm going to die."

The creature charged, however, before it got more than a dozen strides, something flew out of the woods and landed on its back. Siona realized it was the wolf. She screamed. The wolf had the back of the other animal's neck in his jaws. The wolf was digging his claws into the skin and holding on while the monster tried to buck it off, to no avail. Deep red blood spouted from where the claws raked its skin. A chunk of hide flew off when the wolf became dislodged. Instead of attacking, the beast ran the other way. Siona ran to the wolf, who lie panting on the ground. She stood back, checking for new wounds and to see if there was blood from the old ones. He was fine and stood up moments after Siona got to him.

Siona stood where she was, amazed at what he had done for her. He came up next to her and butted his head against her side. She knelt down next to him and he licked her face. She did not know she had even been crying. The wolf butted her again as she stood and she realized it wanted her to walk. She started down the trail with the wolf by her side.

"Are you going to stay with me for a while?"

"He is."

"I think you need a name. You remind me of the wolf on the flag that flies over the castle. Now a name. I think it should be Fenrir. All right, Fenrir let's go home."

27

Chapter 27 - Discovered

The two walked together through the dark woods for some time. Siona noticed there seemed to be more sunshine. As she kept on, the darkness faded and the midday sun shone through. They came across a large clearing that was so bright that Siona stopped to let her eyes adjust. She moved into the open cautiously, but realized quickly that nobody else was around. Siona sat and ate in the sunshine before moving on. She found a spot in the tall grass and leaned on Fenrir, who nudged her hand so that she stroked him. She was so tired she ended up slumping against him and falling into a deep sleep.

The wolf suddenly awakened Siona. Abruptly rising, her head hit the ground. She quickly got to her feet and glanced around, but saw nothing. Then she noticed Fenrir wasn't looking at anything on the ground, he was looking at the skies. She too looked up, although she only saw feathery clouds sailing across the sapphire sky. She glanced down at Fenrir and saw he continued to look intensely at the sky, when he suddenly growled and Siona looked back up. The sun became blotted as she watched. There, to her surprise, was a dragon. The majestic pumpkin color dragon was soaring through the air. Sophie knew the dragon and rider must be from the castle. She yelled, "Down here!" and waved. She saw the dragon circle and come closer.

"Please tell my Papa where I am."

Can you hear what she is saying? asked Tegan.

Noo. Should we move closer? said Gearcleite.

Can you see who it is?

Ay sees a wee ane with a wolf.

Do you think it's the missing girl?

Ay canna tell. We should ga back and tell the others.

Tegan bit her lip and closed her eyes. Some instinct told her this was the girl from the cave. There was no way she could hide this from the Guardian. She was confused and torn about what to do. How did her grandfather not know what was going on? Tegan knew she needed to get a message to him, but she would have to figure out how. Knowing how angry he had been when she left, Tegan wasn't sure he would even listen to her.

Yes, let's start back. Dip your wing to let them know we saw them.

Sophie saw the dragon dip its wing and waved to them. She looked at Fenrir and rubbed his head.

"Well, do we stay or go?"

With that, Fenrir walked to the other side of the meadow, even though he kept glancing at the sky as if he expected the dragon to reappear. Siona wished she knew what was going through Fenrir's head. She questioned if it was the same as what she was thinking. *Would the rider tell someone they saw her, or was she still on her own?*

***

Even as the old man wandered the hills, he couldn't keep thoughts of Tegan out of his mind. Had he been too harsh? Now, as his anger had cooled, he realized that if she didn't come back again, he would be completely alone. If she didn't return this Saturday, he would get word to her through that boy, Carin, or his cousin Nessa. They were always looking for ways to get on his good side. With these thoughts swirling around, the old man entered the cave just after dusk. He lit the fire and made dinner. He kept glancing over at Banprionsa; something did not look right. The braid, it just felt as if...

Lift your wing. I want to see the girl.

She is asleep. Ye leave her alone.

The old man snatched up the bow and knocked an arrow. He knew he had been foolish not to insist that he see Siona. The more he thought about it, the more confident he was that she wasn't hidden under the dragon's wing. Pointing the bow at the ground, he glared at Banprionsa.

Lift your wing now or else.

Are ye going to shoot me?

Right through the wing and if the girl is there, it will kill her.

Ye ga ahead.

When did she leave? Tell me or I will shoot out an eye.

Banprionsa had known this was going to happen, that eventually, the old man would figure it out. She hoped Siona had enough of a lead to make it back before he found her. Banprionsa would not give him the entire truth. Just enough to keep him satisfied. She sighed and glowered at the old man.

She left yestreen.

Which way did she go?

Ay d'noo ken. Ay am not with her.

The old man returned her stare with one of his own. He wanted to lash out at the dragon. However, the look she gave him was so like the one his friend Conall's dragon Galtenga would give him, it stopped him short. He knew Galtenga had mated with another before the war. Their coloring and looks were so similar. He couldn't bring himself to harm her yet. He still wanted to recruit Conall. No, he wanted his brother, Brenn, the Guardian. He was the reason he had lost his dragon, his home, his family. It was the Guardian's fault his daughter had not had proper care and had died. He was the reason that he lived in a cave and not a castle. So, the old man decided he would hold off hurting them for a while longer. It was too late to search tonight. He would go out as soon as the black night changed to orange.

The old man suddenly worried about what the little girl might run into. Good thing he had taken out the wolf. One less thing she might encounter. Why did he care? He had to think of them as if they were the enemy. As soon as this thought flitted through his brain, the one that followed sounded just like Tegan. *How can they be the enemy, they're only children?* With that, he slammed a plate of raw meat in front of the dragon, put the fire out, and took to his bed on the other side of the cave. He would get up early to go look for her.

28

Chapter 28—Dragon Riders

Tegan and Aine sat cross-legged on the crest of the hill that looked down on Dragon Alley. Villagers, castle occupants and dragons had trampled the grass here, so it was nothing more than green hard-pack earth. The two had been there from the moment the first rays of the sun tipped over the trees. Waiting, waiting for the signal they should come down. Hoping today they could go on a real ride on their dragons. Yesterday, they had been the first two to mount their dragons and rode just barely above the ground. If they had fallen, the most that could have happened is they would have bruised themselves.

Aine had brought a freshly baked loaf of dark bread with seeds sprinkled on the top, along with a jar of recently made strawberry preserves and newly churned butter. Tegan had talked the milkmaid out of a small pail that was still slightly warm from the cow. The two girls had been chattering like a troop of howler monkeys from the moment they arrived. Each had only one question they wanted answered. Finally, Tegan could stand it no longer.

"Did you talk to Ferris? Are we going to get to take an actual ride?"

"He wouldn't say yes or no. It is infuriating. All he would say is you'll have to wait and see like everyone else."

Silence descended, sudden quiet like the forest animal when a predator was stalking. Then the Guardian strode from one of the dragon caves, his staff in his right hand, and waved for the two to come down from the hill. They gathered the remnants of their meal and hastened down the hill to join him.

"Good, you brought breakfast."

The Guardian handed Tegan his staff. Her gaze went to the light blue crystal on top and a vine that encircled the oaken shaft, which had six animals carved into various leaves. The eyes were so lifelike that they seemed to peer at her. Meanwhile, Aine had torn off a chunk of the bread and slathered it in butter and jam. The Guardian took a bite and chewed on the fresh bread, relishing the mixture of the newly baked bread with the rich flavor of strawberries and butter.

"You two did well yesterday. Follow me so I can see if we have gear for you. I presume you are up with the roosters because you wish to ride?"

The two nodded mutely and followed the Guardian back toward the dragon cave. Entering, the absolute cleanliness of the place startled them. No sign or smell of mildew or rat droppings that caves often had. No water drops formed on the ceiling waiting for you to look up to land on your face like bird poo. Along both walls were saddles, only recognizable by the strap that would circle around an animal to be cinched up to hold it in place. These saddles were a cross between the most exquisite leather chair and a warm winter coat. Tegan reached up and traced the white wolf that was etched into the dark brown leather. She caressed it like she was actually touching the animal itself. Her finger traced the outline and then reached up to the fur line back. She realized that there was a pouch in the back that she could tuck the fur hood into. It looked like it would hold other supplies, too. Along the side, there was a small open-topped Ascham that could hold a bow and a dozen arrows. It looked as if it would be easy to reach, even when riding. Some straps went from the back of the saddle and attached to others that came from the bottom up. There was one final set of straps that would fit from side to side over the waist of the rider.

"Good choice," said the Guardian, "That belonged to Gearcleite's great-grandmother, and we have checked. It fits her perfectly."

"I get to use this?"

"Yes. Ah Aine, I see you too have found the right saddle too. Now, Riders, before you can go, you need to learn how to get the equipment on your dragon partner."

At this announcement, from behind a burlap curtain ambled in Gearcleite and Tuarcleite. They went to the side of their riders and greeted them.

"Gather the equipment, riders and go to the training area."

"Excuse me, why do you call us 'Riders'?" said Tegan.

"Because we make no distinction between male and female. To avoid this, once we have decided you can ride, we then know you as riders."

With that, the Guardian exited, laughing to himself. He wondered how long it would take them to figure out how to get the equipment off the hooks and out to the training area. He would have liked to stay and watch, but knew it would be better if they did it themselves.

Tegan and Aine stood together, eyeing the equipment. They looked at each other and wondered. They were too short to reach the hooks and there was nothing around to help them lift it down. Gearcleite and Tuarcleite could stand it no more. They wanted to go see this part of the world that was new to them. Before they could speak, Tegan looked at Gearcleite.

Can you reach the equipment off the hook?

Without a word, Gearcleite reached her long neck up and hooked the saddle around her shoulders. She lowered the Ascham down so that Tegan could grab it. When all the equipment was there, they headed out to the training area. Once there, the Guardian had them place all the gear on the ground. They then went over the parts and how each went together. Then came the challenge. Getting the equipment in place. Gearcleite went down as close to the ground as she could. Tegan hefted the saddle up on to her and she stood up. Immediately, the saddle came crashing to the ground. To keep himself from laughing, the Guardian turned away from the girls.

"Keep trying."

"Any tips?" asked Aine.

"Just keep trying."

After several attempts with the same results, Tegan finally asked Gearcleite if she could just go up enough that she could pull the straps together and hold the saddle in place. This took a couple of more tries until Tegan was successful. She cinched the saddle in place and then looked over at the Guardian. She was ready to fly. He walked over and inspected what she had done. He made a few adjustments here and there. Finally, he nodded assent. Aine hadn't seen what Tegan had done to get her gear. Several minutes later, she had her gear. She placed it on Tuarcleite. Then the Guardian walked over and nodded she had done a good job. He told her she could fly around the castle grounds and practice landing. She couldn't leave the immediate area until Tegan was back and he gave her permission. Aine started to argue then stopped. The look he gave her said keep talking and you won't be flying at all.

Circle the ridge about six feet off the ground and then return. I want to see how Gearcleite sits the saddle. Put the back straps on.

Disappointment flitted through Tegan's eyes. However, she nodded and soon with Gearcleite; she was soaring over the ground. Too quick, it ended, and she landed with a jolt, almost losing her seat. Since she didn't, the Guardian told them they could take off, but needed to be back in three hours.

"Go toward your aunt's. But don't land anywhere."

Tegan nodded, and with a stomach full of happy ants, off she went. Gearcleite circled the castle, slowly rising higher and higher. Glancing down, Tegan's mind spun dizzily for a moment.

This is what the eagles see.

As they made their last circle, they went through a cloud for the first time. Tegan became disoriented. It was like she had wandered from the heat of summer into a blinding blizzard, but before the bracken baked on her brain, she was out again. Then she looked out and realized the world had changed. There, perched on the top of a shelf of the cliff, was an eagle's nest. It was longer than twice the length of her arm and so deep she thought she could stand in it and maybe see over the top. It looked like a giant's child had tried to make a basket. The sticks interwoven, so that each ends protruded out. It was not symmetrical. Inside were bunches of grass and moss. There was no bird in the nest and she glanced around. Nearby, soaring above her, was the eagle. It had a yellow beak and legs, black-as-coal wings, the tips of its feathers were snow white. Tegan thought she had seen nothing so striking before.

Hae ye ever seen the ocean? said Gearcleite.

No, someday though.

Let's ga now. Tis noo faur.

Gearcleite took an extended, sweeping circle and headed toward the cliffs. As they approached, Tegan noticed the taste of salt on the air. She could hear thunder coming from below. Then she spotted it, the vast azure nothingness. She saw the wave form then crash and die out as it crocheted white lace on the sand. They flew further out to sea and Gearcleite dropped closer to the water. Breaking waves slapped and caressed Tegan's face with cold salt spray, and she laughed with freedom. She spied the cliffs, surprised at how the snowy bluffs appeared to be painted in charcoal. Lines cut through the whiteness, showing the strength of what the gods had formed.

Sorry, we must noo linger or we willnae make it to your faimlie's home and back in time.

We'll come again soon. Thank you for this. It is beyond what I imagined.

They skirted the castle, hoping that their detour wouldn't be noticed. Gearcleite skimmed the tops of trees and pointed out people and houses to Tegan, who saw them as if they were ants crawling underfoot. She watched as the river she had crossed came into view. She now understood the power of it as she observed the water cascade from the cliff, pounding the rocks below and shooting spray taller than the castle. The dense mist nearly obscured the falls, but she could make out an arching shadow just behind. Tegan asked Gearcleite to circle around once, to check for a place on the cliff face where she might climb down to investigate what she thought was a cave. Gearcleite hovered, and it reminded Tegan of floating in a sun-heated pond. The cares she bore fell like autumn leaves. She never wanted this moment to end. Then Gearcleite tilted a wing, and she saw a dent in the precipice that appeared to provide access to its lower levels. She marked it in her memory for the time she could return and assuage her curiosity.

They gracefully wheeled inland and followed the river's path for several miles. She saw where the banks had been breached and how the trees crisscrossed from side to side. Here the water had slowed. Gearcleite pointed out to Tegan a beaver family gnawing at tree limbs while others moved them into place. She watched as a group of deer came down to the water's edge to drink their fill. She saw a fawn slip into the water and get towed off when a buck charged in, grabbed the fawn by the neck and pulled it back to shore. He pushed it away from the edge with such persistence, Tegan wondered if the stag was worried the water would take the fawn from him. Gearcleite went closer to the ground at the edge of the forest. Tegan watched as a coyote chased down a rabbit who wasn't fast enough to make it to its warren. Though she understood the coyote needed meat, she still felt sorry for the rabbit. She wondered why she had never felt sorry when she caught them for *her* supper.

They headed back to the tops of the trees as they came up to a farm. From Tegan's vantage point, she saw how the farmers laid out their fields. How each farm had several crops growing, but as a whole, they looked like a giant's patchwork quilt of kelly, emerald and hunter greens, with the forest green of the trees stitching them together. She spied a shepherd boy with his staff, as he herded his sheep toward a trickle of water-tinged green with moss-covered rocks. She flew by the woods surrounding her grandfather's cave, wishing she could set down and see him.

Then she flew over to her aunt's small farm, and she saw her brother and sister helping harvest vegetables in the back-family garden.

How close can we get?

Would ye like to land?

You won't tell?

Ye think Ay would tell? The dragon asked, throat tinted orange in mild irritation. *Of course Ay willnae.*

They flew low to the ground and Tegan yelled, "Hello." Her brother and sister looked up and waved with their entire bodies. Gearcleite suggested they make a face in the clouds to entertain the children. Tegan agreed, but quickly pulled on the fur-lined coat attached to the saddle. As they rose toward the clouds, Gearcleite suggested she put all the straps on and cinch them tightly. They were going to do some more acrobatic flying, and she didn't want to lose her rider.

Approaching the cloud, Gearcleite issued a stream of steam that separated the cloud in two. She went to the largest and made a loop around it. As she reached the bottom of the circle, Tegan screeched, then let out a whoop of joy. Never had her heart raced with such excitement. Never had she felt so like she owned the world, never had she wanted something to go on and on. Using her wing tips and the turbulence of its passage, the dragon added ears, eyes, and a mouth to the cloud creature. Then she flew past the farm and swept around so that Tegan could see what they had created. Tegan laughed and clapped her hands. Where there had only been clouds, the face of a wolf appeared. Gearcleite and Tegan landed on the opposite side of the house in a space. Before Tegan could dismount, the children, followed by their aunt, were there. As they saw the dragon, they stopped short and stared with eyes the size of dinner plates.

"You were flying," said Quinn.

"Yes, and it was fun. You looked like bugs I could squish."

The children smiled at her and laughter bubbled up from deep within their chests.

"This is Gearcleite. She and I have become bonded."

At the sound of her name, she lowered her head, as if bowing to the children.

"Can we touch her?" said Molly.

Gearcleite understood the request and lowered her head again, taking a step closer to the children. The children reached up to touch the dragon at the same time. Much to everyone's surprise, the dragon glowed, spilling golden light over the small group.

Tell the wee anes thay hae the power of a rider within them... Someday, thay will find a dragon of thair own who will glow for thaim and thay will bond with a dragon of thair own.

Tegan repeated to the children what Gearcleite had said.

"I saw a picture in my head of us riding; is that what you see?" said Molly

"Kind of, words eventually come with the picture and I can understand what Gearcleite is saying."

"Can I have a ride?" said Quinn.

"Not today. We have to get back to the castle, but we will come back as soon as we can."

At this Tegan give the children and her aunt a hug, then remounted and off the pair went, heading back the way they came. Tegan asked Gearcleite if it was normal for a dragon to glow for someone after they had bonded with another. Gearcleite told her she had never heard of it before and that they should ask what it meant. Maybe, if the rider or dragon died, it was still possible for them to bond with another, so they wouldn't feel the loss so profoundly.

They rode in silence while the wind whistled around them. Tegan's thoughts were on her brother and sister. The life she now had was giving her so much while they continued to struggle. Her aunt and uncle should have children of their own, but as long as Molly and Quinn stayed with them, they might feel like they couldn't have more children. It would be too hard to feed them all. The lightness she had felt earlier vanished and where her heart lived, it felt like a boulder had taken residence. She could ask the Guardian; maybe he would let them come to the castle. There were other young children. Although if she did, it would further anger her grandfather. It wasn't fair.

As they passed the meadow that was just past Tegan's grandfather's cave, she thought she spotted someone other than him.

Can you swing back around? I saw something I want you to look at.

As they turned back around, the person on the ground started waving their arms. Tegan could not make out who it might be. Some instinct told her it was the girl from the cave. *How could that be? He had bolted her to a wall,* Tegan thought.

I can't really see the person waving, can you?

Tis a yung person, noo even as auld as ye. Ay thinks tis a boy because of the short hair. Whoever it is haes a large dog but... No, a wolf.

Could it be a girl?

Maybe. Do ye think tis one of the two that is missing? A stripe of fuchsia curiosity slid down her snout.

I don't know. But don't you think that the girl's dragon would be with her and not a wolf?

Ye need to tell thaim what we saw.

Yes, let's hurry back.

Tegan now had an extra worry. If that was the girl, then how had she escaped? Where was the dragon? Was her grandfather hurt? She wanted to turn around, except if she did Gearcleite would wonder, and how could she explain this to anyone? She was lying to everyone, and it was going to catch up with her. Had her grandfather really stopped loving her? Would they separate her from Gearcleite? Not that — it would hurt too much. They had bonded, and she felt their souls had mingled. To be ripped apart? She would surely lose part of herself. Tegan did not know what to do or who to trust. Like a fledgling that had fallen from its nest, she was lost. Lost in her own thoughts, Tegan did not realize they were back at the castle until Gearcleite let her know they were going to descend.

Hold on, ye d'noo want to fall off.

As she glanced across Dragon Alley, Tegan saw people were being herded out of the way by the Guardian, just as a shepherd moved his sheep along. Gearcleite circled three times before the Guardian waved her to the ground. The landing was perfect and Tegan dismounted like she had done it all her life, rather than a mere half-dozen times. She looked around and saw Aine. The two rushed toward each other and words cascaded out like a waterfall down the mountain cliff. Then they just laughed. In those few moments, Tegan felt like she had when her parents had lived. The world was a special place and she could conquer anything. Aine had more to tell. She shared that someone had sabatoged her gear and she had almost fallen. She told Tegan that the Guardian had used magic to fix it so she could still fly.

"I see you two have much to share with each other, but first I have something for you."

The girls looked at each other, then back at the Guardian. He pulled out of his cloak two long neck-scarves, one green, embroidered with the tree of life, the second was red and embellished with an eagle.

"After their inaugural ride, we present each rider with a scarf from their original house. Aine, they sent this from your king and was the scarf worn by your great-grandmother. Wear it well. Tegan, yours took a bit of research. This scarf is from my family tree and given to me by my brother. We have learned that going back several generations, you and I are related. So, I give to you the scarf my brother gave me."

What the Guardian didn't say was, "you are my great -great-niece." In time, this would come out and Tegan would know that they had a strong family bond. Tegan took the scarf and rubbed the lamb's wool across her face. She looked at the Guardian and didn't see the enemy her grandfather said he was. Instead, there stood someone she might still be a child with, someone who might look out for her, someone she might share her burdens with. Now that she knew they were family, she saw that her brother, Quinn, looked like him. Their eyes were the same shape and color. She wondered what he would look like without the beard. Would he look like her grandfather? She looked carefully at the scarf the Guardian had given her. It surprised her when she looked at the eagle. Her mother and aunt each had a scarf with an eagle that looked exactly like this one. How could it be? She knew Grandfather was older than most people. When he told stories, it was like he had lived several lifetimes. The Guardian had that same look Grandfather did when he was thinking back. Now that she realized they were brothers, it made her wonder how long they had lived. She had heard stories of people who had lived for generations. That they had a special elixir that kept them the age they were. Stories said some of them had helped build Castle Ashwind after the second great war. She wanted to ask the Guardian so many questions, but she knew she would end up telling him about her grandfather. No matter what had happened between them, she would always love him and never want to do anything that would cause him harm.

Ferris came up with two of the softest looking blankets that either could imagine. Each matched the scarf the girls held.

"These go on your dragons so all will know the Houses you serve, but also note that on each there is a scroll to show that all houses are intertwined and that you serve the people of Ashwind."

The girls grinned and hugged each other. In a flash, Tegan's smile fell from her face. She knew if is she didn't tell the Guardian what she had seen, then Gearcleite would mention it and it might look suspicious. With that, Tegan told the Guardian about the person in the glade. She stressed the short hair and that whomever it was had a wolf with them. The two looked like they belonged together. She also confessed that all the times she had ridden that way, she had seen no one in the glade before.

The Guardian looked at Tegan. Though she tried to hide it, he saw the fear in her eyes. He stood for a moment, glancing around the busy alley. Riders taking off and landing. People falling from their dragons because the seats were not tight enough. It all felt normal, like days passed. He knew this was not true for everyone. Here and there, he still saw individuals, almost always adults, scurry around the dragons. Children could be so much more accepting. Tegan didn't take her eyes off of the Guardian as he surveyed the surroundings. She was afraid for her grandfather. Tegan didn't know why, but she had been told this man was their enemy. She had to stop looking for a friend and remember what her grandfather had told her. She needed to keep his secrets, no matter the cost to her. For the second time that day, she felt like she was standing under the waterfall and the full force of its fury crashed down on her head.

"Why don't you show a couple of us tomorrow where you spotted the child? We had best be sure that it's not Siona."

Tegan went with Gearcleite to remove the gear and get it stowed. She didn't know what she should do. She thought about sneaking out that night and riding to see her grandfather, but she wasn't exactly sure where the searchers would be. Tegan was afraid of getting caught, and if she was wrong and it wasn't Siona, she could make things worse. She went to bed late, as the last sliver of the setting moon shone through the window of the room she now shared with Aine. She dreamed she was riding Gearcleite, and that when they landed, wild wolves attacked. Then she dreamed other riders surrounded her grandfather with weapons and that they all shot him at once and dozens of arrows ripped through his flesh. Each time she had one of these dreams, she awoke with a tightness in her head and heart, sweat coursing down her face. She finally gave up and sat on her bed watching the sun and moon play tag before the moon disappeared and the sun took its place.

29

Chapter 29—Banprionsa's Escape

The old man woke early the next morning and grabbed up the bow. He looked over at Banprionsa and thought she must still be sleeping. Without leaving her any food, he strode from the cave. At the mouth of the cave, he stopped. With the wave of his hand, he secured the entry from someone trying to leave or come in. He had been foolish before, and that was how the girl had escaped. He would not be so again.

Banprionsa watched him through lidded eyes as he gathered his things to leave. She had decided in the night that it was time to escape. There was no reason to remain in the cave now that he had discovered that Siona was gone. She had done what was possible to give Siona a head start. Once out, she would circle the sky, looking for her. If Banprionsa found the girl, she would somehow get Siona mounted and fly away. It would be dangerous, but staying on the ground with the old man looking for them was even more so. If she couldn't find Siona, she would continue back to the castle and get the others.

Several days before Siona had left, they had worked on freeing Banprionsa from the wall. Siona had used the knife that she had "borrowed" to cut her hair to work on the rock around where the spike was protruding from the cavern wall. Siona had excavated enough of the surrounding stones that Banprionsa had yanked it the rest of the way out. The only problem was they had created a big hole. This meant that whenever the old man was in the cave with them, Banprionsa had to make sure the hole stayed covered.

Banprionsa was eager to leave, but she wanted to be sure that the old man would not return mid-escape. However, she was hungry and yesterday's kill lay where he placed it. She didn't care that he hadn't cooked it. In fact, it was better that way. Better still if it was fresh. Banprionsa had little choice, so she lumbered to her feet, stretching both legs and wings. It had been days since she had stood. She wobbled a little like a newborn foal, but made her way to where the rabbits lay and ate them, fur, paws and all, without a second thought. Next, she consumed the vegetables. No reason to make it easy on the old man and leave him food. Best if he had to take time to forage before he could resume the search.

She had waited long enough. Banprionsa decided it was time to get moving. She headed out toward the mouth of the cave. As she approached the opening, she didn't understand why she felt reluctant to leave. Her head throbbed as if some spiked fruit was growing inside, pressing ever harder on her brain. It was like a great wave was pushing her back toward the inner sanctum. She retreated around the corner and the pressure on her mind lifted. Banprionsa realized that the old man must have placed a spell on the way out. She retreated further and felt relief. Banprionsa headed back to the more massive cavern and looked around to see if she could find something to help disarm the spell. She looked at the small bow and arrow, but discarded that idea immediately. She thought about taking wood and setting a fire, but wasn't sure if that would cause more harm than good. There really wasn't anything she could see that would help. She was going to have to force herself to move forward, no matter what her instincts said.

Banprionsa wanted to know if she could fly. Had the spell that bound her and kept her from flying worn off sufficiently? Would she be able to do more than just walk? If she could soar, the movement forward would propel her onward and it would be harder to stop. The only way to find out was if she tried. Did she dare? What if she could never fly again? Maybe she should just wait. No, that was not the dragon way. Flying and keeping their friends safe was part of their creed. She had never given up, never waited for others to decide. Dubhbragh was her father, and he had taught her to put others first, to lead. She reluctantly ignored a lifetime of adult injunctions and tried flying indoors. First, she tried just lifting herself off the ground. When that was successful, she rose higher. The first few circles around the inside of the cavern were low, just in case. Then she went higher, dodging in and out among the stalactites, making a game of it. First weaving between them, then seeing how close she could get to their tips without hitting them. Next, a combination of both. In the end, anyone could have heard her laughter echoing through the chamber. With every pulse of her wings, she could feel the blood circulating and flowing to every section of her wings. She landed. A great weight removed.

The time had come. It was now or never. Banprionsa raised herself off the ground and headed down the corridor, gaining speed as she went. She hoped she could take the curves without running into the walls. She rounded the last bend, claws skating across the walls as she used her legs to redirect momentum. The invisible pressure mounted. Banprionsa closed her mind and sped up. She could hear the waterfall and see the sky beyond, freedom a few steps away. She hit the opening, only to be thrown back down the passageway. The spell did more than make you want to stay, it forcibly kept you inside the cavern.

Banprionsa hit the side of the wall, stunned. She just lay there for the moment. She could still feel the desire to withdraw and the building pressure in her skull. The dragon took a deep shuttering breath and crawled slowly back to the entrance. She poked with her claw all around, looking for some weakness. Frustration built up a head of smoke and fire. It snorted out at the entrance only to have it rebound and singe her feathers. With one last bit of will, she struggled up and took several steps back. Perhaps the magic had weakened. It was time to force herself out again. Squatting, claws dug into the floor, Banprionsa readied for a last thrust toward freedom. Suddenly there came the sound of one or more voices. Their source was unclear, but they were getting louder. She quickly backed up around the corner. If this were the old man, he would need to lift the enchantment in order to enter the cave. The only choice was to fly past him. With sufficient speed and surprise, he might hesitate long enough for the escape to succeed.

30

Chapter 30- The Rooms' Help

Cody, the female essence who lived in the beaver room, woke Dalton from a sound sleep.

Go to Westerly's room. We have news of the human girl.

Dalton didn't waste time asking questions or getting changed. He left his room and went down the hall to Westerly's. As he raised a fist to knock, the door swung open and Dalton saw Westerly perched on the side of his bed.

"So, they woke you, too."

"Yep, tell us what found," said Dalton.

"Should we get the others?"

"If needed, they would have woken like did us."

Westerly nodded, and Riley started speaking.

We have found Siona. She is in the woods to the north-east near a waterfall where great magic guards its entrance. She is sleeping on the edge of a forest near a meadow. The searchers need to go into the forest to the north. You need to tell them.

I'll get Aine. She can reach Ainmire, said Westerly.

She has gone on the dragons to search.

I can still try to reach her.

Don't, she is too new to riding. You shouldn't distract her.

"Dalton, any ideas?"

Farah and Tristan practice, said Dalton

As he finished speaking, the door opened and in walked not only Farah, but the rest of the Guides. They all took their usual seats and Westerly explained what they had learned.

"Riley has told us where Siona is and we need to contact the searchers. Aine has left with the group searching this morning. So we have to find another way. Farah, Dalton says you and Tristan have been practicing mine talk."

"We have, but usually we know we're doing it. I'll try."

"Wait, Farah, Tristan and I have been practicing too," said Mirah. "We started right after Siona ran away. We aren't always successful. I wonder though if Farah and I link up if between us we can reach Tristan."

Without saying a word, Farah reached for Mirah's hand.

Tristan had woken before the others and was standing by the river, watching the leaves tumble over the boulders. He wasn't really watching, just staring at it without really seeing when his head started to hurt. Then he felt like someone was knocking on his subconscious.

Leave me alone.

Instead, he felt the knocking grow louder. He slowly realized it was someone wanting to mind talk. He would just tell them to go away.

Go away.

Then he heard what he hadn't expected.

Tristan, listen. We think we have a good idea of where Siona is, said Farah.

Tristan stopped and didn't move, didn't breathe. Could they really know?

T*ristan, are you listening? Can you hear me?*

Yes Farah, I hear you. What do you need?

Send me a picture of where you are. Describe it with as much detail as you can. Mirah says to tell you to say where the sun is coming up and what flowers are near.

The sun is coming up in front of me, which is away from the castle. I'm standing next to a stream.

Where you are is the stream straight or curvy? Is the stream big or little? asked Farah.

The stream curves ahead. Right now the stream is not enormous, but I can tell from water markings that when the rain comes it gets to be very large.

Westerly wants to know if you're near a waterfall?

No, but the dragons said there is one a short walk into the mountains.

Oh, oh, we found you on the map.

Can you find Siona? asked Tristan.

Not yet, will keep trying. We only have a general direction, said Farah.

Tell me. Is the dragon with her?

No, from what we have found out, she escaped, but her dragon didn't.

There is no way she would leave Banprionsa.

Maybe they agreed to it. But that's not important right now.

You're right. Where do you think my sister is?

You need to go to the waterfall and then follow the stream until you can cross it easily. Once you do that, look for a footpath. It's going to be... What's that Riley? Ok I'll tell him. Riley said to tell you that the footpath could be covered in leaves so you might not see it. So instead, look for a place that you can easily walk through the trees. Follow them until you reach the meadow.

I understand. I'm going to get the others going.

Let us know what happens. And keep listening. I'll be in touch if we learn anything more.

Tristan felt his mind empty of the others' presence as he walked over and joined the other group.

31

Chapter 31 —Showdown

As Aine was still sleeping, Tegan dressed quietly and went to the kitchen. There they gave her cheese and bread, which she took with her to a rock on the side of Dragon Alley. From there, she could see both sides of the castle and with a small turn of her head, she could also see the dragon's path to the caves. She sat way back on the rock in a spot that was still cloaked in night so others could not see her. Tegan watched as the workers arrived and headed toward their various trades. She watched as riders snuck out of the castle and over to the path to see their dragons. She saw the two boy talkers, Pogee and Ryuu, stand at the end of the trail and their dragons come to them. Then the boys mounted and rode, doing tricks that if an adult saw them, would most likely keep them grounded for a good long time. She watched them until they realized the sun was almost up and then they snuck back to their home and probably into bed. She finally saw the Guardian. He and his dragon came out at the same time as if doing a dance. They met in the center. Tegan could not hear what they said, but she certainly imagined it.

"Tegan, you might as well join us," said the Guardian.

"How did you see me?"

"Your hair captured the sun. It is like rubies and reflects the sun back at us," said the Guardian.

"When do we leave?"

"The others will be here shortly. Get your scarf and dragon quilt."

"Yes, sir."

As Tegan left, Dubhbragh sent his thought, first to Gearcleite to join them and then to the Guardian.

Do ye think she will warn him? said Dubhbragh.

I think she may. But I'm going to give her that chance. Let her ride in front. Suggest that she land if she meets anyone. I don't think he will harm her, said the Guardian.

Ay agree, he will noo harm her. But do ye think letting her warn him is the best idea? asked Dubhbragh as he walked back and forth a few paces. The only outward sign of his agitation.

Probably not. But I would rather not have to fight Garvin with Tegan watching.

Ye still love him.

No matter what, I will always love him. He is my little brother.

Others had joined, with dragons and riders greeting each other. Still so new to each other, they spent every waking moment wishing they could stay together. Some children had taken to creeping out of their homes and the castle to stay with their dragons. The Guardian knew he needed to stop this and would soon, but right now was not the time.

Pogee and Ryuu came up to the Guardian, their faces expectant.

"We want to join in looking for our sister," said Ryuu.

"Please...." said Pogee.

"Boys, why do you ask when you already know the answer?"

"But, we ride well," said Ryuu.

"If you don't want your mother to find out about the tricks you were doing this morning, make yourself scarce so that in my being busy, I will forget."

The Guardian watched the two boys: first their looks of disappointment, then they turned to surprise and chagrin.

"The day after we get the girls back, as long as your mother and father agree, I will take you on a ride to the beach. Now get out of here before I change my mind."

Everyone had hung back and waited while the Guardian had talked to the two boys. Their antics were only a secret from their mother, and nobody wanted to admit they knew. Once they were out of hearing range, and everyone the Guardian expected had arrived, he outlined his plan. The only part of the plan that Tegan really heard was that she would lead the way to the meadow. Once there, Tegan would land if she saw anyone. If there was nobody to be seen, she would stay in the air. Some others would land to do a search, at which point she was free to go search other areas alone by air. Even though this was good news, Tegan was apprehensive, as if there were caterpillars worming their way down her intestines.

As the Guardian signaled for everyone to mount, Aine rushed up, asking if she could join the search. Ferris told her if she hurried she could come along, but they would not wait for her. Her dragon, Tuarcleite, entered on cue, and she was ready in minutes. It helped that the two boys, Pogee and Rue, were there. They scampered like mice getting the gear in place. With that, they waved her off and Aine rose quickly into the sky and, with the sun beating down on her, she tried to make up the space between her and the others.

Aine passed the main group, looking for Tegan. She saw her in the lead and though she heard the others calling her to stay with them, Aine pretended she hadn't understood, so she could join Tegan. Tegan gave Aine a half-wave when she hailed her, but it soon became apparent that she was concentrating on the ground below. Because Tegan was busy, Aine enjoyed sights she had never seen before. She wished they could go more like a donkey than a hare, but she could tell Tegan was locked in and seeing something ahead that wasn't even there yet.

Tegan was praying to the Gods that she could reach her grandfather first. This group of riders wanted to hurt the person who had taken the children. She could understand that they wanted their children back, but she couldn't allow them to harm him. He said they were the enemy. Why? She just didn't understand. As they approached the meadow, she had Gearcleite slow. Tegan thought she saw someone just inside the tree line. She circled the field with Aine next to them. Aine pointed an arm toward the shadow that moved. It was a man.

"Aine, please circle here and tell the others I've landed."

"I'm going with you."

"No, you need to stay up here."

The man stepped out from the tree line. *How dare they come wearing the scarves of riders?* His brother had the nerve to wear the one he had made for him, and was that an elf with him? Yes, he could make out the green that was usually the color they wore. Well, his time had come. He had always been the better marksman and the Guardian would find out just how good he had gotten at shooting moving targets. After all, deer, rabbits and elk didn't stand still for you to kill them. They might be far away, but he knew he could get him within a few shots.

The old man grabbed up the massive bow and slid an arrow onto its rest. He nocked the arrow, closer to the size of a lance, and raised the bow. Leaning back and tilting the bow just enough to keep the lower limb from touching the ground, he drew, pointed it at the green scarf, and loosed the arrow. He missed, but he saw his brother haul on the reins and swerve to place himself between the other rider and danger. Quickly he nocked another arrow. Tracking him like a dove, he followed the rider's path, determined where he would go next, adjusted his lead and let fly. He hit a leg and saw the Guardian arch backward, then slide toward the injury. The man smiled grimly. Another shot and that should end him. The old man readied another arrow, calculated the lead, and relaxed his hand so that the string slid smoothly from his calloused fingers. He followed the arc of the shaft and the path of his target. There would be no missing this time. He watched as the rider was transfixed, struck above the right hip, the broad-head exited just forward of the left armpit. Flopping sideways in the saddle, a high squeal wheezed from the rider. The red scarf blew away from her face.

"NOOOOOOO!" came out of his mouth like a wounded eagle unable to protect its young.

That wasn't his brother, it was his beloved Tegan. What had he done? What had he done? She was slipping. She slid out of the saddle and only a foot held her to the dragon. The old man stood frozen, his Tegan, his Tegan.

Gearcleite felt the impact of the arrow. The colors of her entire body blanched in unison. She knew it struck Tegan. Gearcleite turned to go back, but felt Tegan shift in the saddle. She twisted her long neck and only saw Tegan's leg. She was losing her rider. This could not happen. She headed toward the ground, knowing the chance was slim that she would make it, as Tegan slipped even further. Gearcleite signaled to Tuarcleite to get below them, so when Tegan fell, that might get her onto the other dragon's back.

Hanging upside down by one leg far above the earth, impaled by a sapling-sized arrow, Tegan knew her time had come. She could feel Gearcleite's frantic twists and turns aimed at keeping her rider from what the girl knew was inevitable. Tegan's foot slipped further, and she jostled painfully against the dragon's flank, the shaft bending and twisting inside her. Tegan knew she was going to fall, and she had no way to save herself. Gearcleite was signaling everything she could think of. Tegan broke into her thoughts.

Promise me you will go to my brother and sister. You will tell them it was an accident. Promise me you will try to bond with one of them.

Ay will promise to go see thaim and try to bond with thaim, but this, it was no accident.

Promise, accident, that is my grandfather. He doesn't know it's me. He must think it was someone else.

Ay promise.

With that, Tegan's foot slipped the rest of the way. Aine reached out for her and their fingertips brushed softly like a bird's feather.

Tegan soared. She put her arms out like she had seen countless eagles do when they wanted to glide on the warm currents. It worked for a moment. She felt as if she was floating, even when she spun head over heels, overhead, arms and legs thrown outward, flapping loosely like a rag marionette. The earth and sky danced round and round her, as if she was some maypole liberated by a tornado. She even floated above her pain. Tegan streaked toward the trees like a burned-out star falling to earth. She knew. Still, a wisp of hope welled as she saw the top of the trees, limbs outstretched as if to catch a baby robin falling from the nest. She strained her arms, reaching and missing each branch, crashing through them like a boulder in a landslide. Tegan was not slowing down at all. She was racing, and the ground was rising to meet her.

Tegan hit the ground with such force that the arrow was ejected from her body and found purchase from a nearby tree trunk. She bounced once and even as her body settled, the old man was by her side, his face like a cliff with water racing down it. He saw her eyes were open, but even as hope flared, he looked over the rest of her body. Her legs and left arm lay carelessly piled about her at angles never intended, more like freshly drowned worms than limbs, bones like broken tree limbs protruded through her skin. His attention was so focused on Tegan he didn't hear the Guardian land only a few feet away.

"Tegan, oh god Tegan, this is my fault," said the old man as tears ran down his face.

"Not your fault, Grandfather,“ weased out Teagan.

The old man had to lean close to hear what she said. He reached over and wrapped his calloused hand around her remaining intact hand. Until that moment, he never realized just how small they were. He always thought of her as capable; she could hunt, dress fish or deer and cook anything. All the things he could do. She could find herbs to cook with or to heal. This she did as if she had been born knowing the plants. She felt them and they had told her which to use and which to leave alone. This child was a marvel and in that moment, he realized he had not allowed her to be a child for a long time. He had dragged Tegan, as if she were a puppy, into his fight and like a pup that wants to please her master, she had done all the things he had ever asked of her. He knew now that he had tried to poison her against everyone but himself. She, though, was like a crystal stream of water nothing could touch. Tegan had done his bidding, but never fell into the trap the bitter old man had tried to lie for her. This was his fault; he knew she had been rushing to warn him that his enemies were coming, that she would die for him and that was precisely the outcome he had caused.

"Grandfather, promise you won't hurt the children." She softly bubbled, "Not their fault."

He nodded his understanding of what she was saying. From the flash in her eyes, he knew she took it as agreement. The old man would let her think about what she liked. He wasn't sure he could give them up now that this had happened to her. He felt a small squeeze in his hand and...

"I love..."

Even that was too much for her small body. He watched as her lids slid closed, like a curtain covering a window. Nothing there now but a shell. The old man thought he could see her spirit depart from her like a puff of smoke from a campfire. He hoped she would pass over and not wander the woods like some. He wanted her here with him, but not that way. Never like that. His beautiful granddaughter was gone, and it was his fault. He should have known it wasn't the Guardian, his hateful brother.

"I love you, Tegan."

The Guardian walked over to his brother and stood on the other side of Tegan. He lifted his face and Garvin saw that tears feel trickling down his cheeks.

"Garvin, I am so sorry. I never thought this would happen. She was a wonderful girl, so much like you as a boy."

"Brenn, can you help her? Save her? Bring her back?" pleaded the old man.

"I'm sorry, after that fall... there isn't anything I can do."

"Are you going to kill me now?" Garvin asked as he stood, his words robbed of all emotion as if he didn't care.

The Guardian looked at his brother sadness of several lifetimes covering his face, like moss on a stone. Didn't Garvin know that, even now, all he wanted was his brother back, that he loved him as much now as when they were children? Yes, they had fought on opposite sides of a war, but that was differences of what they thought was right, nothing to do with how he at least felt.

"No Garvin, I have no intention of killing you unless you force me to. I just want to know where the girls are so I can return them to their families."

"I need you to take care of Tegan, get her to her aunt's, tell Kyna I'm sorry."

With that, the old man got up and stumbled towards the woods. Grief flew off his brother like leaves in a storm. The Guardian knew he couldn't just let him go. He had to stop him. As he started toward his brother, he signaled the others to join him and he felt a windstorm of wings on his back. Ferris dismounted, and he took the blanket from Gearcleite's back and covered Tegan. Just as he folded the blanket over her face, he heard a sob coming from over his shoulder. He realized Aine was there, and that she had seen the broken body of her friend.

Aine sobbed, recounting her failed attempt to catch the falling girl. She was so very sorry. This was her fault. Ferris wrapped the young girl in his arms and held her. He stroked her hair like a mother cat licks her newborn, giving her whatever strength was in him. Soon Tegan's dragon, Gearcleite, pushed her way to the front. Gearcleite's maroon breast radiated waves of desperation and loss. Ferris knew he had to act quickly or Tegan would not be the only causality today. He looked at Gearcleite and told her she would go with the Guardian to take Tegan home.

You will go with the Guardian and take Tegan to her aunt's. He has learned the aunt is pregnant and will offer her a home at the castle. You glowed when Tegan's brother and sister touched you, a thing so rare it can't be ignored. Go bond with them. Care for them, as Tegan would have. They need you.

Gearcleite listened to Ferris and then gently reached down and moved the blanket from Tegan's face. A silver tear fell from her eye, landing on Tegan's face. The salty pearl rolled down the dead girl's forehead. Its track marked her with the dragon flame rune. This would allow them to find each other in the afterlife. With that, she covered Tegan's face and walked to the other side of the meadow, needing for the moment to be alone.

The Guardian grabbed his brother's arm and pulled him around. Before a word could pass, the old man raised his hands and lifted the Guardian from the ground.

"Tegan is dead, and this is your fault."

"Garvin, this is nobody's fault, but I can't let you leave."

With that, the Guardian whispered a few words, and Garvin's hold on him was gone. He landed on the ground like a falling boulder, painfully jarring his spine, but he remained upright. The sunlight strobed as the shadows of the remaining circling dragons swept over them. The two took fighting positions as they had as boys. Both crouched. The Guardian held his hands open at belly level, palms to his opponent. Garvin held his left arm straight out from his shoulder, right fist balled at his hip. The old man circled, and he soon had the Guardian's back to the woods. Garvin knew what he had to do. He needed to grab the elf girl, who stood transfixed by Tegan's crumpled form. She would shield him. There was no way his sanctimonious brother would harm a child to get to him. But he couldn't just grab her. He had to let his stupid brother think he would fight.

The old man raised his hands and a column of power, like hammered lightning, landed where the Guardian had been. It put a hole in the ground the size of a man's head. The Guardian avoided a direct strike, but raised his arms too late. Dirt and stones pelted his face, muddling his vision. While the old man covered the distance between him and Aine in a long bound. He grabbed her by the shoulders and pinned her to him with his arm under her throat. A knife appeared in his other hand and he held it against the vessel that pumped life from the heart to the brain.

"I am going now, with the girl."

Still wiping at his eyes, the Guardian took a step toward his brother, then froze as the knife pressed harder against the Aine's flesh.

"Garvin, I know you remember, so know the one you hold is named Aine. They named her for her great-great grandmother and has the look of her. For the love you once held for her grandmother, I beg you to let her go," said the Guardian.

"I will think about it. But, for now, get out of the way."

With that, the group parted and let them move. The old man stepped into the woods and melted away like snow in the sun. He removed the knife from the girl's neck, but kept her right in front of him. He wasn't sure what he would do. Aine, this child, came from the great love of his life. People now wouldn't understand, but back then, the tribes mingled. It was normal. When he went to the other side, he had lost her. His Aine had not agreed with him. The old man had said hurtful things to her and left her with tear tracks running down her face. The old man knew when he flew away that he had lost a piece of himself, but he made a wall around his heart and placed the love he felt for her inside it. He stopped and grabbed the girl, turning her towards him. He needed to see for himself if the Guardian told the truth or lied.

The hair was different, but those eyes that sparkled like the lake when the sun hit after rain held unshed tears. He saw the same look in them he had seen on the day he left her namesake. The hurt, fear and lack of understanding of what he was doing shown through. Then she blinked and again he saw his Aine. This time the look of defiance, the same one she had shown her king when she announced she would not marry who he had selected for her as a child. Instead, she would marry Garvin. He was the human boy who had been always there in the background, always overshadowed by his brother. The King had looked at the granite in the girl's eyes and acquiesced. Though the old man wanted to take this girl's life, he couldn't. His Aine was there, and he had hurt her once. He couldn't do it again.

"You will stay here. Count until you are tired. Then count again. If you try to leave right away or follow me, you will forfeit your life. There will be no second chance."

Not waiting for her to reply, the old man moved at a speed that belied his age. She watched him jump logs like a deer and shimmy through spaces that should have been too small for a child. Aine did as he asked, except she sent a message to Tuarcleite that she was safe and would return as soon as she could. Aine stood and turned to walk back the way she had come. She had marked the path so that Ferris could follow. Now she could use the small bent branches of trees and plants to return to the others. As she walked, Aine told the plants she had harmed that she would see if they could be made whole. Aine was sorry that she had to cause them harm and only did so to keep herself, as well as others, safe. Aine knew they understood as plants parted like soft butter when a knife was used for cutting. She should have been scratched and bleeding, but she was not. She broke through the forest back into the clearing and saw that Ferris was arguing with the Guardian. When Ferris saw her, he smiled. Within moments, though, he had left to search for Siona.

32

Chapter 32—The Search

Siona woke shivering in the chilly morning air. Fenrir had curled himself around her during the night, so she fell asleep wrapped in fur, but now he was gone. Siona wasn't worried. She figured like last evening, he went off to forage food for himself and would be back shortly. Siona propped herself against a tree and listened for the wind-voices. She realized she had not heard them since sometime yesterday. She assumed she must be safe. Siona pulled her small cache of food toward her and ate some nuts she had gathered as they had walked.

She heard what sounded like a mad bull crashing through the forest, but decided it must be Fenrir warning her he was returning. She smiled and remembered how she had jumped like a scared bunny on his return last night. Then a sound like a wounded animal came to her on the wind. For a moment, she didn't recognize that it was a human voice. As it drew closer, she heard one word repeated over and over: *Tegan.*

Siona listened more closely and recognized the voice, muffled by a black cloak of pain. It was the old man. She looked for a place to hide, but the wall of woods was too solid to penetrate quickly. The small clearing in which she stood contained only one large bush. She whispered to the trees to help her, but nothing happened. She was alone. Siona crouched behind the bush, but knew that she wasn't hidden.

One turn of his head and he would spot her. She wasn't even sure exactly where he was coming from, as the sound echoed in the morning stillness. It was too late when she realized he was heading for her like an arrow to its target. There was no place for her to go. He was going to capture her and take her back to his cave. This time, he would make sure the chains were tight. She squeezed her eyes shut so she wouldn't see him grab for her, but the sound stopped and she popped her eyes open. Siona saw the old man backing away.

He had grabbed an arrow of impressive length and girth that, if it hit her, would skewer her like dinner, with room left on the shaft for a small garden of vegetables. He pulled the bowstring back to his chin, released, and the arrow flew. Siona watched it pass the old oak tree, pass the place where she had slept the night, pass the little mud puddle she had jumped over just minutes before. It felt like the arrow was crawling toward her like a snail. She was dead. She knew it. Then, in a blink, the arrow lodged in a tree behind her. He had missed, but another arrow was already being knocked to shoot at her. Again, he shot and missed, then a third. Still, he missed, but only because she moved slightly to the right. The entire time he shot, his face was marked with pain and tears that just didn't stop. He yelled at her that as his Tegan had died, so would she. Then he would go for the dragon. He screamed after that, he would kill everyone at the castle. He was out of control and Siona had no way to stop him, no way to keep him from hurting Banprionsa or hunting her family.

Siona decided her only hope was to see if she could get him to talk to her. Get him to tell her what happened to Tegan. Maybe she could distract him until he calmed down. She felt his pain like a sharp knife to the heart. The child in her wanted to help him like she had helped the wounded wolf. But the man was far more dangerous. Distracted by her thoughts, she failed to react as another shot came. It grazed her arm and took with it the top layer of skin. It stung and tears filled her eyes. She spun, searching in vain for an avenue of escape that had not been there moments before. Through her cloud covered eyes, she saw two golden orbs fixing her from the velvet shadows of the wood.

Fenrir streaked by her like lightning. He bounded toward the man, who stood stone still with surprise. Fenrir leaped, and the man lurched back, tripped and fell, his head clipping a massive limb on his way to the ground. He was out like a snuffed candle. The wolf stood over the man, his mouth packed with teeth as sharp as dwarves' picks, and descended toward the man's throat. Siona raced like a gazelle to join the old man and Fenrir. She grabbed the wolf around the neck and futilely tried to pull him away from the old man. She might as well have tried to take a cedar for a stroll. The wolf turned its head to Siona and growled as if to say, *stay out of it*. She continued to tug at him and he crept back, as if he was being denied a tasty treat. Siona placed herself next to the old man. His head was bleeding, but his breathing was steady. She knew that if she let Fenrir kill the old man, Siona was no better than him. She had always felt that in the end, he would let them go and he acted this way only because of some terrible tragedy.

"Let him be. He can't hurt either of us right now."

Fenrir looked into Siona's eyes and howled like the moon was high in the sky. His answer was not an unqualified *yes,* but an understanding that now was not the time. Siona needed to decide what to do. Did she head back toward the cave the way the old man had come? Maybe there had been a battle and people would be there. Maybe her father was there, or the Guardian. Or perhaps it was a trap and she would end up worse than she was now. She gathered his bow and arrows, shouldered the oversized weapon, so it didn't drag on the ground and headed to the main path. There, Siona paused. First, she looked the way she had been going. If Siona continued that way, she would head into the unknown. Then she looked back toward the curve in the path from where she had come.

"Which way?"

The wolf went on alert, his tail went up and his body down, poised to strike at the new threat he heard. She grabbed the bow from her shoulder and tried to bring it to a firing position. The massive wooden arc was too long and the lower limb struck the ground. She tried to hold it horizontally, but it was too heavy to keep at arm's length. Frantically, she looked around her. A lightning blasted tree stump crouched near the trail, raising two truncated limbs in surrender. Using both hands, Siona lifted the bow over the limbs so that it rested parallel to the ground with the bow on the far side and string on her side of the trunk. She nocked one of the broom-length arrows and, holding the string with both hands, heaved back. Leaning against the weight of the bow's pull, she dragged the bowstring back as far as she could and hooked it onto the notch of a sapling. She picked up a solid-looking stick and slid it into the notch below the string. So, a lift of the stick would allow the string to slip from the young tree and launch the arrow.

Siona only had time to wipe her sweating brow when a group of men came around the corner. She had one hand on the wolf and the other ready to release the arrow. The wolf let out a growl as loud as a dragon's roar. Everyone coming around the corner froze in their tracks and even the birds forgot to sing. Silence reigned while they appraised each other. Then someone spoke.

"It's a boy with his wolf. Never seen the likes of that before."

Without thought or care, Siona let loose. "I'm not a boy."

From the back of the group, a boy pushed aside those that were in front of him. He alone seemed to recognize the voice. Tristan reached the spear-point of the group and saw Siona looking like a warrior prince, bow at the ready and hand on a gigantic wolf. He looked from Siona to the wolf and took a step forward. A long low growl emitted from Fenrir's throat, his teeth bared and he bent his hind legs ready to spring if any came near.

Siona stared at the boy in front. She couldn't believe he was here. Siona had stopped believing her brother would come. She gently plucked the arrow from its perch and let the bowstring lose. She bent down and whispered into Fenrir's ear that this was her brother and he wouldn't hurt her. That this was the person she had been searching for the past few days. The wolf turned its massive head toward her. Everyone stopped breathing. Fenrir licked the tears that trickled down her cheek. Siona stood up, but kept her hand on the wolf's head. She moved forward, first a couple of tentative steps and then, as fast as a hare could go, she closed the distance. Fenrir stayed right at her side.

Something unfroze inside of Tristan and as she ran toward him, he moved to meet his small sister. He grabbed her up and held her to him, raining kisses on the top of her dirty, matted hair. Never had a sight been so welcome. She was safe, his little sister. A whimper came from the wolf and he looked up at Siona. She squirmed and her brother put her down. She tugged him down onto his knees so she could introduce her friend to him. Confused, the others stood ready to intervene if the wolf attacked.

"He won't hurt me or anyone I tell him not to. I saved him after the old man shot him with the arrows and he has stayed with me so I could find you. He saved me from the old man just a few minutes ago."

"Where is the old man?" said Ainmire.

"Over there. He hit his head when Fenrir jumped on him. His head was bleeding, he was unconscious, so I took his bow and his knife, then left."

At that, Siona pulled out a knife from inside her waistband. The knife was so huge it surprised the men she hadn't cut herself. He had made the knife from Damascus steel with whorls like crashing waves and with a rose-colored elk horn handle. Few had seen any with craftsmanship like that.

"May I look at it?" said Ainmire.

Siona shrugged and handed it to him.

"This is elf made. I've seen very few like it before. It's very valuable."

Again, Siona shrugged.

"You can have it. I don't really need a knife like that. Just don't give it back to the old man."

"I will hold on to it until you are older. You might change your mind," said Ainmire.

"Did you find Banprionsa?"

"There is another group looking for her, but can you show us the way?"

"I don't know for sure, but I crossed a meadow. Wait."

Once more, Siona leaned down and whispered in the wolf's ear. He looked at her, cocked his head and made some whimpering sounds that were eerie coming from a beast that large. It sounded like a dog whose master had abused it. Siona stooped further down and put her head right on top of his. She sat and pulled his head into her lap, where she stroked it and explained that the men would not let the old man hurt him again with the arrows. But she needed him to help her find her friend who the old man had tied up in a cave. Tristan knelt down next to Siona and the wolf. He, too, spoke to the magnificent beast who looked up at him with wary eyes, as if he didn't really trust what the man was saying. Fenrir clambered to his feet and nudged Siona, who also stood. He stretched out and stalked toward the men who had waited, still huddled in a group. They scattered like birds from a pouncing cat. He neither looked right nor left, but with Siona by his side and her brother right behind, they proceeded down the path.

***

The Guardian watched as the first group moved out of sight. He turned and looked at those who waited for his instructions.

"Aine, I need you to stay here."

"But I can help."

"This is not the time for a discussion."

"Let me at least go into the forest and talk with the trees. They should be able to tell us where the old man lives."

"Alright go, but we won't wait long."

Aine didn't follow the group that had just left, instead slipping through a gap between two saplings. She walked away on ground covered in leaves that had not been trodden on for years by any of the two-footed races. She knew what she was looking for: not the juvenile trees that were forcing their way up from the earth searching for the warmth of the sun. Not the adolescent who wanted to stretch their branches to show they belonged. Not even the adult who, though still moving towards the heavens, were content with their lot. She sought the ancient ones who had stood on earth so long that the follies of man no longer surprised them. Those would be the ones the tree from the Elf Alter would communicate with. The others might know, but they were still selfish and often gave misinformation and laughed as the seekers looked in the wrong direction. But Aine was getting impatient; she feared the Guardian would call her back before she could find the ancient ones.

She stopped in a clutch of trees and skipping the youngest went to an adult tree asking if it knew where the old man's home was or at least point the way. It surprised Aine as she pressed against it to feel fear, like acorns drop from its branches. She pleaded with the tree to give up the information. But all it would say to her is *go away, leave us alone, go home.* Those words echoed through Aine's mind as if she stood in a canyon and had yelled the words across to the other side.

Aine didn't give up. She couldn't. Aine needed to find Siona, yes, but she also, perhaps a little selfishly, felt a deep desire to prove herself. She moved forward and brushed against an oak shoot just peeking out of the ground. The bare skin of her ankle had touched it and she heard a word. *Wait.* It shot through her veins. She stopped and sat cross-legged in front of the sprout. Gently, she reached her hand out and embraced the small trunk. The tree told her the Ancient One said to walk three hundred paces to the north and then forty to the east. It waited there for her. She thanked the young tree and wished it good fortune, strong sun, cool rain, that it would rise to the sky like the clouds and always be as strong as the stone of the earth.

Aine followed the directions precisely and found herself in front of a tree more gnarled than the hoariest crone. She saw where in the past, a woodsman had tried to fell it. The ancient tree was magnificent, its bark was weathered like the side of a cliff where waves had carved their stories. Aine felt the power of the tree and gently placed her palm on the trunk. She asked permission to speak, and it was granted. She told the tree of the brief battle and of Tegan's fall from the sky. Aine told of the missing girls, one human and one dragon. She assured the Ancient One that they were not here to hurt him or other creatures of the woods, only to find their missing friends and take them home.

The old tree listened and knew the truth of the girl's words. But she hesitated. The old man who she spoke of had been good to them, keeping away the woodcutters and those who would hurt them. He had been a friend to them and had taught his granddaughter their ways.

Aine would not give up. She explained Tegan was his granddaughter and that her last wish was that the children would get safely home. They would not harm the old man. Tegan's death was too much for all of them. They only hoped that nobody else would be hurt. The tree was silent. The forest held its breath.

Then the Ancient One spoke. The Ancient One told Aine that the old man lived behind the mist, that there he dwelt in a cave that had been made by his rendering an opening large enough to enter a great hollow in the earth. She told of the woods around and how they had helped one small being escape from there. She was not sure about the winged creature if it still was there or had bolted through the skies.

They spoke for a few more moments, then Aine heard her name being called. She thanked the old one and asked if could she do anything for her before she left. The old tree let loose a shower of acorns and asked her to plant a grove by the castle so it would have roots that traversed the distance. She asked Aine to return and speak to it of the world outside their realm. Aine promised all the ancient oak had asked her to do would be done and then headed toward the sound of her name.

Aine met the Guardian at the edge of the meadow. She told him what she had learned and showed him the seeds she had received and the promise she had made. Without hesitation, he told her they would, of course, honor the request. With that, he signaled the others to mount, and they flew into the cloudless blue of the sky.

33

Chapter 33—Fathers and Grandfathers

The Guardian and Dubhbragh led the others, skimming the tops of the trees. With the description Aine provided, he knew the region of the forest where they needed to head.

He spotted a mist and Dubhbragh reached out to Banprionsa, hoping he could connect with her mind. But what happened left him shaking. Not only had he not been able to reach her, but he had entered a void. There was no sound echoing back to him; he had felt no creatures. He insisted they land as soon as they could. Dubhbragh saw a small clearing, and the Guardian told Conall and Galtenga to join them. As he banked, he told the others to circle and keep watch. To spread out and see if they could find Siona now that they knew she wouldn't be in the cave.

Dubhbragh landed, but not the graceful swan landing, as was typical. He hit an invisible wall of power that batted the pair backward. He had to force himself through. The Guardian helped by cutting the wall with a spell, but it didn't make it easy for any of them.

Yer brother haes learned new spells. Do ye think tis dark magic?

No, he just turned a repel spell up to more than I have ever seen.

So, an auld trick.

Seems like it. I'm going to head toward the mist. I think you should stay here.

No, she is my adopted dochter, said Dubhbragh, the plating of his body flashing an angry orange striated with a frustrated blue.

Yes, I know.

Thay're comin too. Ye may need help. He commanded, his narrow brow radiated cyan.

As they walked toward the cave, the spell sucked each step down, like walking in a swamp. The closer they came to the cave, the more their minds had to fight the desire to turn around. They heard the thunder of the water as it pounded on the rocks below and knew if they fell, nobody could save them.

The Guardian halted them and spoke with the wizard, Conall. They huddled heads together and shouted over the roaring of the falls. Conall suggested they take up opposite sides, one near the water and the other near the trees. Conall's dragon, Galtenga, would fly just next to the rim in case the spell pushed him over.

They rigged a harness with vines from Conall to Galtenga. Then the two took out the wands they rarely needed and back to back paced off the distance that they thought it would require. Once at the proper range, they turned simultaneously like dancers that had practiced for years together. They pointed their wands at a predetermined spot just right of the waterfall. They whispered the words, "*Et tu iubes transeamus.*"

A green and blue streak met, blasting the spell apart. The blast caused Galtenga to be pushed further away from the ledge until it yanked Conall from the cliff and he dangled in midair. Galtenga was free-falling, taking Conall with him. Conall screamed Galtenga's name and just as his hip hit the first outcropping, Galtenga pulled out of it. Conall felt as if someone had shoved an ice nail into his hip. The old man had poisoned the rocks. Galtenga flew back to the ridge just as the Guardian made it to the edge, sure that he would see their broken bodies below him.

As soon as Galtenga lowered Conall to the ground, he collapsed. His hand reached to where he felt the pain in his hip. The Guardian pushed his hands away.

"Don't touch it," said the Guardian.

"He poisoned the rocks," said the Wizard Conall.

"No, I don't think so. Place your hands under you and don't move. There is a rock shard lodged in the bone. This is going to hurt."

The Guardian used a cloth to grab the shard and pulled the rock out in one swift movement. As he did, Conall screamed like a wounded animal. The Guardian used his wand to cauterize the wound even as the pus ran. He was going to close it, then stopped when he realized it needed to drain. Conall had passed out.

While the Guardian attended to Conall, Dubhbragh had reached through the hole in the spell and tried to contact Banprionsa. Though Dubhbragh felt something, it was like hearing an echo dying in a canyon. He felt certain she was behind the waterfall, ice-filling his chest like fire. He feared she could be close to death.

As soon as the Guardian finished, they moved Conall to the edge of the woods. Then the Guardian and Dubhbragh moved on alone. They quickly found the mouth of the cave. The spell here was weaker, and the Guardian blasted it away with ease. It was a straight shot from there to the inner cave where Banprionsa should have been. Dubhbragh called out her name before entering.

Banprionsa turned her head and huffed out the stream of fire she had prepared to let loose on the old man. Then she bounded toward Dubhbragh. They embraced, and both talked at once.

You two can talk outside. I don't want to leave Conall for too long, said the Guardian.

Hae ye found Siona? asked Banprionsa.

Thare is another group searching for her. Ay am sure thay will find her, said Dubhbragh.

As they made it to the back of the waterfall, Dubhbragh stopped. He signaled the Guardian to go on. There was something that he needed to speak to Banprionsa about alone. How was he to tell her that her grandfather was out there? He was so afraid that he would lose her after all this time. He loved her as if he had fathered her and the moon rose and set with her.

My grandfaither is here?

Aye. He came as soon as he was told ye were missing.

Ay feel the bond. It n'er felt like this between ye and me.

Ye should get to ken him.

Ay will. Ay am very fortunate to have a faither and grandfaither to love me. Now, how can Ay get the most out of that?

Dubhbragh snorted mirth-purple fire, melting the nearer stones. He should have known he could never lose his daughter to anyone. With that, they moved beyond the curtain of water and heard laughter and shouting. Banprionsa flew the few hundred feet to where Siona stood. They were free and could go home.

34

Epilogue

The Guardian, Dubhbragh, Siona, Banprionsa and Gearcleite landed in front of Tegan's aunt's house. The children were the first out the front door, eagerly looking for their sister. She had promised a ride on the dragon. Their faces fell when she wasn't there. Tegan's Aunt Kyna came more slowly out the door. She knew something was very wrong.

"I am Brenn, Guardian of Ashwind. I have sad news today."

"Where is Tegan?" said Kyna, her voice sharp as a whip cracking.

"Tegan..." said the Guardian as he stopped short voice cracking,

"She's dead."

"Yes."

The two spoke more about what had happened. Tegan's Aunt Kyna kept looking strangely at the Guardian through her tears. She had seen that face, those eyes. She asked Quinn to join them and looked from the familiar face of her nephew to the stranger standing before her.

"The two of you have the look of family."

"Yes, so we do. I guess you should know. Your father is my brother. We hadn't spoken until today. Not for many lifetimes."

With that, the Guardian looked away and off into the distance. He turned back to Kyna and gave her his proposition. He would like the family to move to the castle where the children would go to school and learn to be riders. She would have a home and work. They needed a gardener with her skills. The castle had many mouths to feed, and they needed someone with her talents. Kyna listened to him, but wasn't sure.

Gently, the Guardian took her hand.

"You know he won't be returning. I know they told you about the bandits that killed him."

He then said that if she wanted to stay, he would be sure she had what she needed, but he hoped she would take on his offer.

While the Guardian spoke to Tegan's aunt, Siona talked to the two children. She told them how sorry she was about Tegan's accident. Siona explained that she and Banprionsa had learned from Gearcleite of the great love Tegan had for them. Then she surprised them by asking if they would each touch Gearcleite. Quinn went first and they could see a small glow, like a candle shine. He pulled away and after a moment, Molly touched the dragon. Again, Gearcleite glowed only a little. Gearcleite then asked Siona to have them link hands and touch her together. When they did, Gearcleite radiated. At that moment, something inside the dragon sparked back to life. She would never forget Tegan, but she now had twin souls inside her. According to lore, this happened only once in every four or five generations. These two would be powerful riders, and it was up to Gearcleite to make sure they were worthy.

Though they couldn't ride, Banprionsa and Gearcleite let the children scramble up onto their backs. Unlike many riders, the two seemed to know instinctively how to mount a dragon. Though the family was sad, the idea of living at the castle and learning to be riders took some of the sadness away.

That night, Kyna saw the fire flicker, as if someone was trying to contact her. She reached over and said the words to let the fires connect. On the other side was a woman she didn't know. Emmair introduced herself, telling her she was in charge of the school's welfare and that three of her children were guides. She also told her that Siona was her daughter and that she had two younger boys. Then she explained she had some sad news. That Kyna's husband's body had been found and would be in Ashwind tomorrow. She received permission from Kyna to have the casket made there and ready for the funeral.

The next day, the Guardian returned and Kyna had packed up the belongings that she wanted to take with her. They placed the children in front of Conall and the Guardian for their first dragon ride. Kyna's eyes were wide with apprehension, but also no small measure of excitement, as they helped her onto Gearcleite. They flew into the bright afternoon brilliance to a chorus of whoops and squeals from the first-time riders.

As they came upon the castle, their mood became more somber. They spiraled to the earth as they neared Dragon Alley. There, they dismounted and walked to the burial grounds. There were two fresh graves. Next to each lay a casket, open, waiting for the moment to be closed and placed into the earth. Molly and Quinn walked with Gearcleite to the first casket that held their uncle, their aunt Kyna's husband and then to the one with Tegan. The children reached up and touched Gearcleite as much to provide comfort as to receive it. Gearcleite shined like the morning star.

They lowered the caskets as they offered prayers to the Gods. Then, as children do, Molly and Quinn wanted to know when they could ride the dragons again.

As Tristan smiled at his sister, Siona, he noticed a dwarf had ridden in and was waiting on the hilltop of Dragon Alley. He gestured for Farah to follow him. As she was talking with Shaun, he came along too. When they arrived, it surprised Shaun was to see the Master of the Dwarf Council, Keagan. He dismounted and walked toward them as he smiled in greeting.

"Are you Farah?" asked Keagan.

"Yes," said Farah.

"I was ordered to give this to you. The old woman said you would know what to do with it," said Keagan. Much to Farah's surprise, he handed her a small scroll. "She said to add good luck."

Without another word, Keagan mounted his horse and rode away.

The End

Dragon Talk

English	Dragon Speak
actually	actilly
against	agin
agree	gree
appraised	apprized
are not	arenae
aren't	arna
argue	argie
away	awa
blood	bluid
bury	birrie
Can't	canna
changed	cheenged

change	cheenge
child	wee ane
come here	cumhere
coming	comin
could	coud
dare	daur
daughter	dochter
Didn't/don't	d'noo
does	daes
doesn't or does not	daesna
down	doon
everyone	aabodie
family	faimlie
far	Faur
father	faither

figure out/determine	suss
friend	freend
gone	gaen
gather	gaither
giving	giein
go	ga
going	gaun
good luck	g'luck
has	haes
hasn't	haesna
have	hae
have not	hinnae
haven't	hinna
heard	haurd
himself	himsel

I	ay
I don't	Ay d'noo
I'm	Ay'm
if	tis
if	ef
just	jist
know/understand	ken
leader	leadiest
live	leeve
love	loo
loved	lood
make	mak
minute	meenit
miss	amiss
more	mare

mother	mither
nearest	naurer
needn't	needna
Never	N'er
nobody	naebody
not	noo
often	aften
oh or other exclamination	ACH
old	auld
Over the way	owerby
said	sayn
Should not	shouldna
someone	somebodie
Something	sommit
sound	soond

speak	speik
take	tak
their	thair
them	thaim
there	thare
they	thay
tomorrow	the-morn
trouble	tribble
us	hus
View	vyow
Wake	wauk
weapon	wappin
we shall	we'se
well	weel
were	wur

what	whit
who	wha
who is	wha's
why	whitfor
will not	willnae
yes	aye
you	ye
your	yer
young	yung
yesterday	yestreen

www.ingramcontent.com/pod-product-compliance
Ingram Content Group UK Ltd.
Pitfield, Milton Keynes, MK11 3LW, UK
UKHW040959030225
454602UK00001B/158

9 798988 056430